Bigsby

By
Dan Snow

ACKNOWLEDGEMENTS

There are many people that had a hand in bringing this story together. First and foremost was my wife Linda, known in our Cowboy Action Shooting circles as "East Coast Filly". She was always there with encouragement and suggestions, and spent many, many hours reading the drafts. One of many reasons I love her.

Tom "Forty Rod" Taylor first gave me the idea that a short story I was working on might be worth expanding into a novella. He was always ready to answer questions or give advice. Thanks Tom.

Tom "Joe Darter" Morris was another inspiration, offering story suggestions, and offering advice on elements to add to the story.

Several folks took the time to read various versions of the draft as the story was developing, and I offer my thanks to them all.

Dan "Clay Mosby" Snow

ISBN 978-0-6151-5102-1

Chapter I

The sun had just started to paint the bellies of the clouds stacked up over the Sierras while a coyote in search of its next meal was trotting along the bank of a dry creek bed. The sound of iron striking rock brought its head up, ears and nose searching for the source of the noise. Movement on the far bank caught its attention and the coyote froze under the branches of a small live oak. Eyes shining, it watched the horse and rider pass, heading down slope towards the valley. The horse was moving slowly, finding its own way. The rider, slumped in the saddle, clothes covered with dust, was staring at something only he could see.

The trip across the Sierras had taken longer than Bigsby had planned. Heading west after stopping at Virginia City to change horses, it had taken only two days to reach the lake where the Donner party had been trapped. It was getting over the summit that had almost killed him. A late May snowstorm moving in as he was climbing out of the valley caught him above the tree line with freezing temperatures and howling winds. Forced to retreat, he'd spent the next two days huddled in a small cave under some tumbled boulders. With very little dry wood for a fire, he'd damn near frozen to death before the storm broke. It'd taken another two days to get over the summit and out of the snow.

Exhausted and out of food he'd finally reached the lower western slopes where he shot a deer. Roasting some strips of venison over a small fire he'd watered and brushed down his horse before staking it out in a patch of grass. After he'd eaten he laid out his bedroll, checked his Colt was close at hand, and fell into a troubled, fitful sleep. He rose before dawn and continued down towards the valley, driven by the message in the telegram.

Bigsby had been working for Colonel Goodnight, driving cattle from New Mexico to the Palo Duro Canyon in Texas when the telegram had finally caught up with him. Bigsby had gone still, his face pale beneath the wind burned wrinkles and dust as he read the message from his father. Handing the telegram to the Colonel, he picked up his saddle and gear and headed for his horse. Reading the telegram, the Colonel uttered a curse than called out to Bigsby, "I suggest you take Lassiter and Big Jake with you."

Bigsby looked at the Colonel. His voice was hard as he said "Thank you Sir, but you're going to need every hand to get these cattle the rest of the way to the canyon. I feel bad enough leaving you like this, but you know this is something I gotta do!"

"I know son, I'd do the same in your place. We'll get the cattle through; you go on and take care of things in California. When you get everything settled, your job'll be waiting for you." The Colonel could see the determination in Bigsby's eyes before he turned to mount his horse.

Now, two months later, Bigsby was making his way out of the Sierra foothills towards his family's ranch near Dry Creek. The fourteen hundred mile trip from the Texas panhandle had worn him down, killed two horses, and used up a good half dozen more. Beneath the wild beard and worn out clothes, the hard miles had turned him rawhide tough; only the determination burning in his eyes gave any sign of the passions that drove him.

Chapter 2

Topping the ridge behind his father's ranch, he stopped his horse in the shadows, only his eyes moving as he scanned the small valley below, searching for any sign of danger. A small stream wound across the valley floor, passed near the three room house, then emptied into Dry creek. The cabin showed new wood where one wall and a corner of the roof had recently been replaced. A bare frame next to a pile of sawn boards stood in place of the remembered barn. A new fence enclosed the corral, and as he watched, a figure in jeans and a home spun shirt hammered together a trough for the horses. Smoke rose in a small curl from the stone chimney of the cabin and he could make out a few clothes on a line between two saplings in the yard.

Continuing to watch, Bigsby realized what he wasn't seeing; cows. When he'd last been here there'd been almost a hundred head in this valley. His father was selling beef to the miners, and doing pretty well for himself. So well in fact that he had been planning to buy some land in the next valley and expand the herd. Now, except for a handful of milking cows in another corral, the valley was empty.

Satisfied, Bigsby tapped his horse in the ribs and started down the slope. As he splashed across the stream, the horses in the corral whinnied. He watched as his father stood up and, one hand shading his eyes, reached for the Winchester close by. Knowing he'd be hard to recognize after the rigors of the trip, Bigsby stopped several yards short. Keeping his movements slow and his hands in sight, he stepped down from his horse. Taking off his hat he finally spoke; "Hello Pa. It's me, Bigsby."

"Bigsby, it's so good to see you again!" Voice tight with emotion, his father dropped the rifle and hugged his son in a fierce grip. "Becca is going to be so glad to see you son."

"She's ok? She's alive? The telegram only said she'd been hurt and it didn't look good!"

"Your mother's a strong woman. Doc wasn't sure at first if she was gonna make it, but after a few days the fever broke and she started to mend. She'll have a limp and a few scars, but otherwise, yeah, she's ok. She's over to the Wendell's place right now; I expect she'll be back in a few hours."

"That's great news Pa! But what exactly happened here? And where are all the cattle?"

"Put your horse in the corral and then come on to the house. I'll get some coffee going and we can sit and talk. It's a long story." Picking up his rifle, Bigsby's' father watched his son for a moment before turning towards the house.

As they sat across the table from each other, his father recounted what was becoming an all too common story in the foothills. Men had swarmed into the region by the thousands, brought by the siren call of the yellow metal being found in the streams and rivers. But it also brought in those that were all too happy to let others do the back-breaking work of panning, sluicing and digging for the gold. They found it easier to get the gold with a gun instead of picks and shovels. Claim jumping, robbery and murder flourished as more and more men moved into the area. Gangs began to form, preying on miners working remote claims in the valleys and canyons. One of the meanest was a gang of outlaws run by Jesse Stewart. Utterly ruthless, his gang was said to be responsible for half a dozen murders, two dozen robberies, and who knew how many beatings. Over the past year they'd begun to extort money and supplies from the ranchers and farmers in the area, threatening violence if their demands weren't met.

"Your ma was in the house and I was in the barn when Will Joslin, John Freeman, and Glen Damon rode up. I knew they'd started riding with Jesse Stewart's gang, and figured they were here looking for trouble," his Dad said. His face was dark as he remembered.

****

"Morning Mosebee," said Will, disrespect evident in his voice.

"You men have no business here, so I'll ask you to leave," Mosebee replied, standing close to the edge of the barn door. He'd been expecting a visit from Stewart's gang after hearing about attacks on his neighbors so he'd been keeping his Winchester close where he could get to it fast. Seeing the three men riding in he had an idea he was going to need it.

"Why now, that's a pretty mean thing to say. We just came by to give you a message." Will held his rifle across the saddle, the muzzle not quite pointed at Mosebee's chest.

"And what message would that be?" Mosebee asked, though he already knew the answer.

"Well, you got yourself a nice place here Mosebee. Got a pretty wife, good sized herd of cattle, seems your doing alright for yourself. Now you know there's some pretty bad people runnin' in these parts, been robbin' and murderin' folks, and nobody seems to be able to do nuthin' about it." Damon was looking pretty smug as he talked; one hand on the bandoleer across his chest.

"Jesse Stewart has decided that something has to be done about these outlaws, so he's formed an Association offering protection to folks in these parts," said Will. "For a small fee we'll make sure these outlaws leave you alone."

"What you mean is if we pay money to that murdering bastard he'll leave us alone. You're no Association, you're just a gang of thieves and murderers, and I'm telling you again to get off my property!"

"You don't really want to be this way, Mosebee. Stewart might not think too kindly of you." The threat was evident in Will's voice. "In fact, I think we'll just have to give you a little example of what might happen. Might help you make the right decision about joining our Association." Will turned his head to look at the two men he'd ridden in with. "Freeman, how about if you and Damon see how strong Mosebee made that corral fence."

When Will turned back he saw Mosebee had his Winchester in his hands and it was pointed at his heart.

"There may be three of you, but you'll never leave here alive if they try anything Joslin. Now get out!"

Staring into Mosebee's eyes, Will went cold. He was going to die if there was any shooting, and he wasn't ready for that. Keeping his hands away from his guns he told Freeman and Damon to back down. "This ain't over Mosebee!" snarled Will. He'd been backed down, and there was no way he was gonna let that go. "You wait, we'll be back, and we won't be so friendly next time!" Viciously pulling his horse's head around, Will spurred his animal towards the road; Freeman and Damon close behind.

****

"I knew Will Joslin was a braggart and a coward, so I figured that was the end of it." The regret in Mosebee's voice was evident as he looked at his son. "They hit us three nights later 'round midnight, four of 'em, all wearing masks. They drug Becca and me out into the yard and then fired the house and barn." Slamming a fist on the table, Mosebee stood up, the rage plain on his face. Walking over to the shelf, he took down a bottle of whiskey. Bringing it back to the table, he poured a shot in their cups. "One of the horsemen rode Becca down as they were riding out, and I got clubbed from behind. When I came to, I got Becca into the wagon and took her over to Doc

Barton's place." Mosebee sat back in his chair, looked at the whiskey in his cup for a long moment, then jumping to his feet, threw it across the room where it shattered against the wall. "By the time I got back here the cattle were gone, scattered over half the county. We finally rounded them up and stashed 'em over to Tinkers' place."

"Was it Stewart's gang?" Bigsby asked.

"Yeah, it was them, but I have no proof" answered Mosebee. "And without proof there wasn't much the sheriff could do. They tracked the horses for a couple of miles into the mountains before losing the trail."

Bigsby found himself gripped by an anger stronger than anything he'd ever felt before. His pa had taught him about honesty and hard work when he was growing up. He'd taught him that when you gave your word you kept it and you gave an honest days work for a days pay. You didn't go looking for trouble, but you didn't back down if it found you. And if someone needed your help, well that's what you did, you helped them out.

"Pa, let me take care of this. You take care of Ma and get the place fixed up while I find Handsome and Calaveras." said Bigsby, standing up to put a hand on his fathers shoulder.

"Last I heard, Handsome was working for Art Delaware in the Gold Creek Saloon and Calaveras was helping John and Angie," replied Mosebee.

"Handsome's working for someone? This I'll have to see for myself!" exclaimed Bigsby.

Chapter 3

It was late afternoon before Bigsby started out to find Calaveras. Ma had come home from the Wendell's and after a somewhat tearful reunion, had insisted that he have something to eat. If nothing else, Bigsby had learned that arguing with his Ma was a plumb waste of time. He watched as she bustled around the house getting things ready. She had a slight limp from a broken leg, and he'd seen the scars on her arm from where the outlaw's horse had stepped on her.

When he'd told her his plans to go after the men that had attacked them, she hadn't said anything, but he could see the concern in her eyes. Becca knew that out here men often had to make their own justice. She just wished it was someone other than her son that had to do it. And she was worried about her husband. Mosebee hadn't said anything to her, but she knew he was still looking for the men who had attacked them that night.

Bigsby was thinking hard as he tied his bedroll to the saddle and double checked the straps holding his Winchester in its scabbard. Far as he knew, this Jesse Stewart and his gang had no idea he was back. If he could keep it that way for a while it'd work to his advantage. He couldn't take 'em straight on, there were just too many. But if he could get Handsome and Calaveras Bear to throw in, the three of them just might be able to come up with a plan that could work.

Heading north from the ranch, Bigsby let his horse pick its own trail over the ridge. Keeping close to the trees, his eyes constantly searched the country around him. Occasionally he'd stop in a patch of shadow and check his back trail. It was only about twenty miles to the Lathrop place from his folks, but that was over some pretty rough country. The foothills were giving way to the higher slopes, an area covered with steep canyons and rushing streams. It was a tangled mix of oak, sugar pine, and manzanita and of course blackberry thickets were all over the place. He figured it'd be late tomorrow before he got to John and Angie's place and found out where they had Calaveras working.

Calaveras Bear; Bigsby had to smile thinking about the first time they'd met. He'd been all of about twenty, and was given the task of driving a herd of cows up to the ranch from the stockyards in Sacramento. Being as how he was young and full of himself, he waved off any offers of help and headed east with forty head. Three days later he found himself south of the Cosumnes River, with the cattle scattered over about six or seven square miles.

He'd about ridden his horse to death, was hungry, bone tired, and madder'n could be. To top everything off, the bull had gotten itself mired in a mud hole, and it'd taken all afternoon to get the stupid thing out. He was sitting on the edge of the mud, cursing the bull, his horse, the weather, and just about anything else he could think of when he realized he wasn't alone.

"Before you finish up there, son, you might want to save a few of them curses for yourself." The voice was deep and kind, but Bigsby could hear the laughter in it as well.

"And just why would I want to do that?" Bigsby said. Turning around to look at the stranger, Bigsby saw a tall cowboy astride a sturdy roan. From his worn chaps to broad brimmed hat, Bigsby had the feeling that this fella knew his business.

"Well, I've been watching you since yesterday, and figured that eventually you were gonna need a hand. Cattle aren't all that smart, and they don't listen very well either. Soon as I saw it was just you trying to get these critters wherever it is you're going I knew it was just a matter of time."

"Matter of time till what?" asked Bigsby, getting a little riled at the laughter he heard in the stranger's voice.

"Till you had the cows scattered all over the hills and realized you weren't gonna be able to keep 'em together." The stranger was smiling now, and Bigsby had to admit he had a point.

"Don't suppose you'd be willing to help?" he asked, getting to his feet and sticking out his hand. "Names Bigsby, my folks have a ranch over near Dry Creek, mile or so out of Drytown."

Stepping down from his horse the stranger took Bigsby's hand. "Folks call me Calaveras Bear, probably because of where I'm from and my size" he said.

"So where'd I go wrong?" Bigsby asked.

"The herd'll follow a lead bull, but you gotta keep 'em moving during the day. And you need a hand or two to keep up with the ornery ones that want to wander off or don't feel like walking anymore. If the bull stops or gets hung up in mud or brush, the herds gonna head off in all directions unless you keep on 'em."

"Can the two of us get 'em back together?"

"Sure, might take a day or so." said Calaveras. "First, we'll drag some branches over to that pocket and make a rough corral, and then we can round up the strays and keep 'em in one place while we get the rest."

It was early afternoon the next day before they had all forty head in the corral. Calaveras suggested they wait till morning before starting them up the trail to the ranch.

"We'd only get a mile or two before dark, so might as well keep 'em together here and head out in the morning".

"I thank you for the help Calaveras" Bigsby said. "I'd probably be chasin' them darn cattle into next month if you hadn't happened along."

Taking the makings from a shirt pocket, Calaveras rolled a cigarette and lit it with a twig from the fire. Leaning back against his saddle, he nodded acceptance of the thanks while taking in a lungful of the tobacco smoke. "Glad to be of help Bigsby. Man sees another fellow in trouble, he's obliged to help out if he can. Been working with cattle for a few years now and I've managed to learn a thing or two about 'em."

"That's what my Pa is always telling me" Bigsby replied. "He's always ready to help folks that need it, and never asks anything in return. Sure he might take something in trade once in a while, but usually it's just a handshake and "Your welcome".

"Your Pa's a wise man" Calaveras said. "And now it's your turn to watch out for predators, both the two and the four footed types. Wake me in four hours and I'll take over."

They'd gotten the cattle to the ranch three days later, forging a strong friendship during the trip. Over the next couple of years they'd worked together a few times, and had helped each other out of scrapes with the thieves and bullies following the miners in search of gold. Bigsby knew Calaveras would be ready to help out this time too, but as he walked his horse below the ridge line to hide his silhouette, he was concerned about the dangers they faced.

Chapter 4

A days ride southwest of Bigsby's camp, Stan Merrill and Slim Wilson had just bedded down their herd for the night when two riders approached the camp. From the look of them they were hard men, and their lathered horses looked about done in.

"Evening Gentlemen, we just got the coffee going. Pedro will have biscuits and beans ready soon, so you're welcome to join us if you've a mind to," said Slim.

"Thanks, don't mind if we do,' said Red Peters as he stepped down from his horse. "This here's my partner Josiah. We've ridden a long way today and appreciate the offer of a meal. Perhaps we could turn our horses out with yours tonight so they can get some grass and a little rest?"

"Sure boys. Gary, take their horses down by the creek and turn 'em out with ours." A young boy looked to Slim when he said this, then walked over and took the reins of the tired looking horses while Red and Josiah stripped the saddles and blankets and dropped them near the fire.

"Where you boys headed?" asked Stan as he poured coffee into the cups they pulled from their saddlebags.

"Looking for a town called Murieta, supposed to be a little north of here," answered Red.

"Yeah, I know of it. They been having a lot of trouble with a fella name of Jesse Stewart from what I hear. Just follow this creek upstream about five miles and you'll come to a fork. Murieta's about another half days ride up the south fork," said Stan.

"Much obliged," said Red.

"If you boys are lookin' for work, we could use a couple extra hands to get this herd up to Redding," said Slim.

"Not interested," growled Josiah, the first words he'd spoken since they'd ridden into camp.

"No need to be rude Josiah, he was just askin'," said Red. "No thanks, Slim, we've been promised a job by a fellow in Murieta. He's buying up some property around there and hired us to help take care of things."

"Buying property in Murieta, heh?" chuckled Slim. "Nothin' there but rattler's 'n cows, people there'll probably think he's daft."

"Don't much matter to us what they think about it," said Josiah. "Mr. Francis's payin' our wages to protect his interests."

"Francis, you say? Haven't heard of him before. He been there very long?" asked Stan.

"Settled there last spring's what I hear," answered Red. "Mr. Francis's from down around the New Mexico Territory, and I heard Texas before that. Anyway, who's this Jesse Stewart you was talkin' about?"

"He's an outlaw that's been preyin' on the miners and ranchers in this area," said Stan. "He's got him a gang of fifteen or twenty that hides out up in the foothills. Hear he's just smart enough to keep one step ahead of getting' caught. Got folks so scared they're afraid to say anything."

"Far's I can see, that ain't our problem," said Josiah. "Now if he was to try 'n bother Mr. Francis, then I guess we'll have to just take care of him."

Watching the two men finish their meal and turn in, Slim briefly wondered what was in store for the folks in Murieta. He turned to look at his partner, "Well, they'll be gone in the morning and we can keep this herd headed for Redding. From the sounds of things, it might not be too healthy around here for a while."

Chapter 5

Bigsby woke up before the eastern sky began to show signs of the coming day. Lying quietly, he listened to the sounds of the forest for any sign of danger. After a few minutes he quickly got up and started a small fire under the low branches of a pine. The thickly laced branches would hide the smoke and the surrounding bushes would hide the flame. With no wind moving the pre-dawn air someone would have to be real close to smell any thing. He put a small pan of water on to heat for coffee while he gathered his blanket and got his bedroll tied to the saddle.

When the water began to boil, he threw in a small handful of coffee and set the pan aside to brew. He quickly put out and covered the fire, and sat with his back to the tree, watching the trail he'd ridden up the night before. Eating a biscuit his Ma had packed for him, he sipped carefully at his coffee so as not to stir up the grounds in the bottom. Finishing his breakfast, he poured out the grounds from his coffee and stowed the pan in his saddle bag. Stepping into the stirrup, he mounted his horse and moved quietly out onto the rocky slope.

Just before he'd stopped to make camp last night, Bigsby had had the feeling he was being watched. He'd circled back, waited, and had seen nothing, but the feeling had persisted. Now, as he moved slowly between the trees, trying to find softer ground to muffle the sound of his horse, he again had the feeling he was being watched. Stopping in a small stand of saplings, he listened, and realized it was too quiet. Moving slowly and quietly, he thumbed the leather straps off the hammer of his Colt and slid his Winchester from its scabbard.

Keeping his eyes moving, it was almost fifteen minutes before he saw a shadow moving where there was no wind. Listening hard, it was another ten minutes before he heard the rattle of pebbles against leaves. He had no idea who was following him, but if they were being this stealthy then they probably meant to kill him if they could. Sitting on his horse, he realized he'd waited too long to dismount. If he moved now he'd give himself away. They didn't know exactly where he was, which was keeping him alive for the moment.

Another twenty minutes went by before he saw a flicker of movement off to his left. Slowly shifting the barrel of his rifle that way, he saw the flash to his right just as the bullet smashed the rifle from his hands. Grabbing his pistol, Bigsby dove from the saddle, rolling under a nearby manzanita.

"I killed him" shouted a rough voice from the trees about thirty yards away. "Hit him in the chest and saw him fall!"

"Then you go in and drag him out so I can see" answered a high thin voice Bigsby recognized. It was Cole Benning, one of Jesse Stewart's outlaws. He didn't recognize the other voice, but at least he now knew there were only two of them. Lying as if dead, he waited for their next move. Hopefully they'd be dumb enough to walk in together, where he might have a chance.

"All right" answered the first, "He ain't movin' around so I figure he's dead. You come in on my left and let's see if he's got anything worth takin' before we ride back."

Bigsby listened to the sounds they were making as they worked their way towards him. He could see the stranger as he approached, but Cole was just out of sight to the left. Timing it to the noise they made, Bigsby slowly thumbed back the hammer on his pistol.

"Put another shot in him, make sure he's dead" shouted Cole. Watching through almost closed eyes, he saw the stranger stop about five yards away and raise his rifle. Knowing it was now or never, Bigsby fired, the slug hitting the stranger in the chest. Not looking to see if he was down, Bigsby rolled to his right, firing the second shot where he thought Cole was standing. As he fired he heard the vicious whine of a bullet past his face, and then saw Cole grab his stomach and fall forward onto his face.

Turning back to the stranger, Bigsby saw him lying on his back, a shocked look on his face. He stood up and walked over; saw the man was dead, shot in the heart. Walking back over to Cole, Bigsby reloaded his Colt. He rolled the outlaw onto his back with his boot and found he was still alive. Looking at his wound, Bigsby knew the man was dying.

"Why were you after me?" he asked.

"Bounty" whispered Cole, his face twisted in pain. "Jesse Stewart was gonna pay one hunnert dollars to whoever brought you in dead. Knew as long as you was alive you'd be after him for what happened to your folks. Guess he didn't want to be lookin' over his shoulder all the time."

Here was the proof he needed to get the sheriff to act, but Bigsby knew Cole would be dead in a couple of hours, if he lasted that long.

"Bigsby, it hurts something awful" moaned Cole. "I know I'm dyin', so shoot me, don't let me lie here like this."

"I oughta let you suffer for what you did to my folks!" Bigsby said quietly. Picking up Cole's pistol, he opened the cylinder and removed all but one bullet, then placed it where Cole could see it. "I'm riding on now Cole, you can lay there and die, or you can pick up this pistol and be a man for once in your miserable life."

Bigsby got to his feet and walked back where his horse stood, head down, grazing on a patch of grass. Picking up his rifle he saw that the stranger's bullet had grazed the stock tearing out a gouge about three inches long. Sliding it back into the scabbard he stepped into the saddle and started down the trail. He'd gone about fifty yards when a pistol shot echoed through the woods behind him.

****

The sun was half way down the western sky when Bigsby rode up to John and Angie's place. John was at a big stump beside the house splitting a mess of firewood for the stove, while Angie was in the house working on some leather for a customer of theirs.

Burying the blade of the ax into the stump to keep it from rusting, John stretched his back, then shook out a bandana and wiped his face.

"Afternoon Bigsby," he said, "didn't know you were back. Last we heard you were riding with Goodnight in New Mexico."

"I was until two months ago" Bigsby replied. "Pa's telegram caught up with me in Texas, took me this long to get here."

"Sorry about what happened to your folk's son," said John. "How are they doing, they need any help?"

"There doing fine John, thanks for asking. Pa could use a hand getting the new barn built and won't admit it, but otherwise I think they're doing ok" answered Bigsby. Taking off his hat he knocked some of the trail dust off his vest and chaps while walking up to shake John's hand. "I came here looking for Calaveras Bear" he said, "and got jumped by two men just this side of Cedar Creek, near the rock slide."

"What!" exclaimed John "You alright? Any idea who they were or what they wanted?"

"What they wanted was me dead." Bigsby said. ""I'm fine, but both of them are dead. I didn't recognize one, but the other was Cole Benning. Just before he died, he told me Jesse Stewart had a bounty out on me for a hundred dollars."

"We thought it was Stewart's gang that hit your parents, but there wasn't any proof." John's voice showed the frustration folks were feeling in not being able to put Stewart and his gang out of business.

"With Cole dead, we still don't have any, but that isn't going to stop me" said Bigsby. "Can you tell me where Calaveras is? I need to find him, and then let the sheriff know about the two outlaws that jumped me."

"Calaveras finished up here and headed towards Murieta this morning. Said he was gonna stop there for a couple days, and then go on into Sacramento. Don't worry about the bodies. We'll get them buried for you, and take their gear into the sheriff."

"I appreciate that John. I was headed to Murieta myself, so I'll catch up with him there." Tipping his hat to Angie who had just come out on the porch, he mounted up and turned his horse west. Even with the head start Calaveras had, Bigsby figured he could catch him by cutting across the ridge to pick up the trail again near the road to Murieta. Not knowing how many more of Stewart's thugs were out there hunting him, he'd have to concentrate on staying alive and finding his friends. .

Chapter 6

Handsome Longfellow looked at his cards and put the best disappointed expression on his face he could muster. There was over four hundred dollars on the table, and the rube across from him was convinced he was going to win this hand. He'd played the game straight in the beginning just to keep in practice, but his current victim was such a bad player he'd finally decided to manipulate the cards so the poor sap could win a little of his money back. Of course that was just to set him up to lose it all on this hand. As he picked up the deck to deal the final cards, Handsome felt a large hand come to rest on his shoulder.

"Now what have I told you about that, Handsome?" whispered Art Delaware. As the owner of the Gold Creek, he'd caught Handsome cheating at cards one day, and had seriously contemplated breaking his fingers before Handsome had been able to convinced him he'd stand to profit from not doing so. "I can run a clean game and bring folks into the saloon," he'd told Art. "You give me a table by the back wall and I give you ten percent of the take."

"Alright," answered Art. "But the first time I catch you cheatin', I'll bust your hands and throw your butt in jail."

In the months that had followed, Art had grudgingly admitted that Handsome had indeed been good for business. He'd kept the card games clean, made an honest tally of his winnings and made sure Art got his share. Folks liked to come in to play where they got an honest deal and bought more whiskey and beer in the process. Sure, there were times when Art knew Handsome was conning some poor sucker, but as long as it was kept out of the Gold Creek and no one got shot, he was inclined to look the other way.

Looking up at Art; Handsome's face twitched a little as he swallowed nervously, "Why Art, whatever are you talking about? Surely you're not implying that this game has been anything other than fair?"

"Let's just see that it stays that way." Art said. "Tell you what, hand me the deck and let's just see if Pete here is lucky tonight." Taking the deck from Handsome he expertly dealt the requested card to Pete, then the two to Handsome.

"Well Pete, looks like Art was right, today is your lucky day," growled Handsome as he looked at Pete's winning hand. "Gentlemen, that's it for today. Congratulations on your excellent fortunes, and perhaps we will be fortuitous enough to meet again in the future. Maybe even in a place with fewer interruptions!" This last was aimed at Art as he walked back behind the bar.

Gathering up the cards and carefully counting his money, Handsome put aside Art's cut and folded the rest into the inside pocket of his vest. Standing up, he adjusted his cuffs carefully before walking over to the bar.

Handing the money to Art, he picked up the offered shot of whiskey, and with a mock salute, took a sip before setting it back on bar. After all, Gentlemen did not indulge in the rude behavior of tossing the whiskey back like a man dying of thirst. This place may be wild and uncivilized, but he was determined to keep up appearances.

"Thought we had an agreement, Handsome," Art asked. "You keep the game clean and I let you keep your fingers attached to your hands."

"Why Sir, how could you possibly accuse me of such behavior?" Handsome asked, managing to look hurt and haughty at the same time. "That gentleman happened to be winning, as you plainly proved when you barged in like a hooligan and interrupted our game."

With just a hint of a smile under his bushy mustache, Art shook his head. "Let's just say that I was trying to help you not make a costly error in judgment, and I'm sure you'll remember this in the future."

"Well, I suppose you expect me to thank you. I don't know why I continue to labor here under such unwarranted supervision," said Handsome, pretending to be quite put out.

"Probably because I've got the only saloon around this part of the territory you haven't been thrown out of, yet!" answered Art.

As Handsome was thinking of a proper response to this he glanced in the mirror behind the bar. Coming through the door behind him was someone he hadn't expected to see for a long time. He was quite pleased to see his friend Bigsby walking up to the bar; but to maintain a proper air of breeding he mustn't show it.

"Well I'll be damned Bigsby. I thought you were out in New Mexico workin' for Colonel Goodnight," exclaimed Art, reaching out to shake hands.

"I was, until I got the telegram about what happened to my folks," Bigsby answered. "Got back a few days ago and talked to my folks. Then, two days ago, I got jumped by a couple of Jesse Stewart's men. Unfortunately for them, they're both dead. John Lathrop was going to bury 'em and notify the sheriff while I came here to find Calaveras."

"Sounds like you still have a knack for getting yourself into trouble, Sir," said Handsome, turning to look at his friend.

"And it sounds like you still haven't learned to keep those aces in your sleeve," said Bigsby. "I can't believe Art hasn't thrown you out in the street by now."

"Wouldn't want to frighten the ladies, now would I?" replied Art. "Sorry to hear about your folks Bigsby. Stewart's gang has gotten people real scared around here."

"Thanks, Art," said Bigsby as he turned to look at Handsome. He'd met him a few years ago when Handsome'd ridden into town; fresh from getting run out of Sonora, they'd later learned. After narrowly avoiding the same fate here by "volunteering" to help them run off a small band of thieves, Bigsby and

Handsome had become friends. It was a prickly relationship at times, Bigsby trying to curtail Handsome's predilection to running schemes on hapless victims, and Handsome making sure that Bigsby remembered things he'd done for him. In spite of this, they knew they could count on each other, and in the end, that's what really mattered.

"I came here looking for you and Calaveras," Bigsby told Handsome. "Pa told me the Sheriff's hands are tied without any proof, and like Art says, Jesse Stewarts's thugs have the folks around here so spooked no ones gonna say anything."

"You're quite correct about that," Handsome replied. "When the possible consequences of speaking out are serious injury or death, there is very little incentive for the people to volunteer information."

"Then I guess it's up to us to stand up for the rest of them, isn't it?" Bigsby asked.

"Somehow, when I saw you walking through the doorway of this establishment, I just knew that imperilment was walking with you," Handsome retorted in the long-suffering tone that only he could manage.

"You can always sit this one out, if you think it's too much for you to handle," answered Bigsby with a slight smile.

"And deprive you and Calaveras Bear of the benefit of my incisive intellect and wit? Without me along you two would most likely succeed in getting killed before you even got started." Looking fully satisfied with himself, Handsome finished his drink, straightened his waistcoat and adjusted his hat.

"Calaveras is staying at the hotel. Perhaps we should join him there, and you can buy us one of their wonderful meals while you try to explain how we won't get shot for our troubles," said Handsome, heading for the door of the saloon.

"I guess I'd better go with him and keep him out of trouble, Art," said Bigsby, turning to follow his friend out the door.

"Bigsby, Jesse Stewart and his gang are not something you want to mess with," said Art. He's got a lot of men, and most of 'em is just down right mean."

"We'll be careful Art, but this has gone too far. The Sheriff can't do anything, but I'm betting we can. If we get the proof he needs, he can start putting these outlaws behind bars." With that Bigsby followed Handsome through the doors of the saloon.

Stepping out into the dusty street, Bigsby heard his name called and looked back over his left shoulder. A tall, mean looking fellow was standing next to the water trough. Seeing Bigsby looking at him, he slowly began walking towards the middle of the street, stopping about twenty yards away.

"Been waitin' for you to show up Bigsby," he said. "I heard Jesse Stewart's payin' a hundred dollars to the man that kills ya, and I figure to be the one that collects."

"Hello Max, never expected to see you again," said Bigsby. Keeping his movements slow, he slipped the thong from the hammer of his Colt.

"Do you know this nefarious looking specimen, Bigsby?" asked Handsome as he prudently took a step to his right.

"Afraid I do," answered Bigsby. "His name is Max Teague. He was a gun hand for a bunch of rustlers that made the mistake of trying to steal cattle from Colonel Goodnight. They hit us one night north of the upper Canadian River in New Mexico."

"We would've had them cattle if that damned Mexican hadn't tipped you off," snarled Max. "Now, I mean to have that bounty, so you best be makin' yer peace right quick"

"Did he talk this much when he was rustling cattle?" asked Handsome. "If so, then I can see why their endeavors were not that successful."

"You shut your mouth, Mr. Fancy Britches." There was a nervous, mean look to Max that Bigsby didn't care for at all. Watching his eyes, Bigsby realized he was going to have to kill him. The man was beyond reason, thinking only of the bounty Stewart was offering.

"Far as I know, I have no quarrel with you Max. Walk away and you can live, keep pushing and you'll die where you stand." Turning to face Max squarely, Bigsby seemed relaxed and confident.

"Quit talking and draw Bigsby!" yelled Max as his pistol cleared leather. He couldn't believe it when he saw the flame explode from the muzzle of Bigsby's

Colt and felt the slug tear into his belly. Desperately trying to raise a gun that was suddenly very heavy, Max never felt the second shot that hit him in the chest and knocked him back against the trough. He hung there for a moment then dropped face down in the street.

"You have such an amazing way with people," Handsome observed, walking back to stand next to his friend.

"I hate killing, Handsome, but he left me no choice," said Bigsby.

"Oh, that was without a doubt the case, my friend, but I'm not the one that needs to be convinced. I see our beloved sheriff coming this way, and he has a particularly jaundiced view of folks leaving dead bodies in the street." Brushing dust from his sleeve, Handsome turned and headed towards the hotel.

Sheriff Martin was a tall lean man with an easy going manner. Folks tended to discount him at first meeting, which suited him fine. Growing up in the harsh world of the western deserts, he was always aware of what was happening around him, and a quick mind allowed him to put things together other folks might miss. This had been a real asset since he'd become the sheriff of Murieta a couple years back.

"You must be Bigsby," he said, offering his hand. "Rumor has it there's a hundred dollar bounty being offered for you. Nobody's talking but its pretty obvious Jesse Stewart is behind it; which could explain why you're standing here next to the body of one of his men."

"You're right Sheriff, and this fellow didn't give me any choice," said Bigsby taking the offered hand. "I've only been back a few days and this is the second time somebody's tried to shoot me. That sort of thing gets old real quick."

"That's what I heard this morning. Mind telling me your side of what happened the first time?" asked Sheriff Martin.

"Two of Jesse Stewart's men ambushed me a couple days ago, above Dry Creek. If their first shot hadn't hit the rifle I was carrying I'd be dead. They got careless and I was able to get them both. John Lathrop was going to bury them for me and bring their gear into town."

"Angie was in this morning and told me about it. I expect John will be here this evening or tomorrow morning with their horses and gear," said Martin. "I've been gathering evidence against Jesse Stewart, trying to get enough to put him away before things get too far out of hand."

"One of the men I shot was Cole Benning," said Bigsby. "Before he died he told me about the bounty, and Max here said the same thing before he drew down on me. I had to shoot to defend myself."

"I know, I saw what happened from across the street," said Martin. "I was coming to find you and see if we could work together on this."

"Then join us in the hotel Sheriff, I'm meeting Calaveras and Handsome to come up with a plan to take care of Stewart before more innocent folks get hurt."

"All right," said Martin. "I'll do that. Let me get this body taken care of and I'll meet you there in thirty minutes."

****

Calaveras and Handsome were sitting at a table near the back of the dining room when Bigsby walked in. Walking up to them he was surprised at how little Calaveras seemed to have changed since he'd left for New Mexico a couple years ago.

"Well Bigsby, I certainly hope you've gotten better at handling cattle than you are at stayin' out of trouble. You've been back what, about a week, and already three men are dead!" Calaveras looked at his friend, marking the determination in his eyes to see that justice came to those responsible for what had happened to his parents. "Seems to me we ought to just let you be and in no time there won't be a gang left for Stewart to lead."

"Good to see you too, Bear," replied Bigsby. After shaking hands with his friend he poured himself a cup of coffee from the pot on the side table and then took a chair with his friends. "I noticed the old Wilson place as I came into town. Looks like someone's fixin' the place up," he said.

"Fellow by the name of Clay Francis rode in here a couple months ago," answered Handsome. "He seems to have persuaded himself that Murieta is going to start growing and is buying up property where ever he can. He's had several men working diligently to fix the place up. Personally, I think the man is daft to be throwing that much money into this town."

"What do the townspeople think of this?" asked Bigsby.

"Haven't heard of anything specific mind you, but there have been rumors that some of the property owners got some pretty rough treatment at the hands of Mr. Francis's men. Mr. Delaware actually tried to block the sale of the Weaver place when he heard that. Obviously, he was unsuccessful in that endeavor, since the Widow Weaver took the money and moved back to Nebraska to live with her niece."

Tipping back in his chair, Bigsby looked at his friends while he drank his coffee. They were still catching up on what each other had been doing when the Sheriff walked in a few minutes later. Bigsby's friends had told him about Sheriff Martin, and from what he'd heard the Sheriff was tough, smart and fair. He'd be a good ally in the coming fight.

"Sheriff, isn't there anything you have you can use against Jesse Stewart and his gang?" he asked.
"So far it's all been second hand, someone told someone who told someone else, that sort of thing," Sheriff Martin answered. "Until you came back and were threatened directly, that is."

"What about the attack on my parents?" asked Bigsby? "Wasn't that proof enough?"

"I was your father's word against theirs, and they all had alibis for the night your folks were attacked. We couldn't track the attackers, so we had nothing the Judge would listen to." Sheriff Martin's voice was calm as he faced Bigsby. "Now we have the two attacks on you, and we have witnesses that heard what Max Teague said about the bounty. I'm trying to put together a posse to go after Stewart and his gang, but so far I haven't found anyone willing to go along."

Looking carefully at the Sheriff, Bigsby could see there was something more than what he'd said. "I can't believe every man in this town is too scared to ride on a posse Sheriff. What is it you haven't told us about yet?"

"Stewart's gang has a hideout up above Indian Diggings," replied Martin. "The town was burned out a few years ago, and a fellow name of Charles McLane owns most of what remains. There are caves and abandoned mineshafts in the cliffs above the creek. From up there a lookout can see anyone approaching. We'd never be able to get a posse near 'em without being seen."

"Indian Diggings you say? That's a few miles south of where John and Angie live. Let's talk to John when he gets into town, see if maybe we can find a way in Stewart doesn't know about," said Bigsby.

"Bigsby, you're not seriously planning to go up against this despicable band of ruffians by yourself?" asked Handsome. "You may be good with that gun, but I do believe twenty to one odds are a bit steep, even for you."

"Not planning to do it alone Handsome. I figured to ask the Sheriff and Calaveras to join me." There was a slight smile on Bigsby's face as he watched his friend.

"And what about me, my dear fellow?" said Handsome.

"Heck, I figure he didn't ask you because it'll involve horses, sleeping on the ground, eating cold grub, and possibly getting shot at," said Calaveras, grinning at his friend. "We wouldn't want to disturb your fine sensibilities by exposing you to such barbaric conditions." As Handsome contemplated a suitable caustic reply, Calaveras turned to Bigsby. "Just what do you have in mind?"

"From what I've seen of his men, it sounds like Stewart's probably the only one in that gang that can think or plan past the next meal. I'm betting that if we can take him out, most of his gang will turn tail and run. Those that don't, we can round up later," said Bigsby.

"Just because I happen to be a gentleman, does not mean I'm unwilling to fulfill the obligations imposed upon me by honor and friendship," stated Handsome haughtily. "I'm quite capable of handling such situations."

Chuckling out loud, Bigsby stood up from the table. "Handsome, why don't you and Calaveras head over to Fiddletown's store and get supplies. I figure two or three days worth should do it. You can have Sally at the livery stable keep an eye on them till we're ready to leave, and ask Bryce to check our horse's shoes."

"You can be pretty sure Stewart's got someone in town keeping him informed of things," said Sheriff Martin as he pushed back his chair. "I'd suggest we don't say anything where we might be overheard."

"Good Point Sheriff, we'll keep that in mind," said Bigsby. "Handsome, Calaveras, when you're finished, join me at the Sheriff's office. We'll wait there for John and then we can make plans without eavesdropping ears nearby."

Chapter 7

Clay Francis was sitting at his dining room table, glass of whiskey at hand. Red and Josiah sat across from him, having arrived that afternoon. Clay had filled them in a bit and was lighting a cigar when he heard the back door open. He had his new nickel plated Remington .44-40 revolver out and lying on the table when Loomer came into the main room, hat in hand.

"Evenin' Mr. Francis," said Loomer.

"What is it Loomer?" asked Clay.

"Was just over to the hotel and saw the Sheriff talking to several men."

"Names, Loomer. Do you have any names for these men?"

"It was Calaveras, John Lathrop, Handsome and Bigsby, Mr. Francis"

"And who is this Bigsby?" asked Clay.

"He's Becca and Mosebee's kid, been over to New Mexico driving cattle for Colonel Goodnight." answered Loomer.

"And just why do you think this information is of any possible interest to me?" Clay had heard about Bigsby, and the attack on his parents. Could he be here because of that, or was it for another reason? This was something he needed to find out.

"They was all talking real serious and quiet like, like they didn't want folks to know what they was talkin' about!" Loomer kept twisting his hat around and around as he he talked, looking with longing at the bottle on the table.

Taking a dollar from his vest pocket, Clay tossed it to Loomer who grabbed it greedily out of the air. "Don't tell anyone what you told me Loomer, and for your sake don't let anyone see you coming in here!"

"Yes sir Mr. Francis. Won't no one know I was here." With that Loomer hurried back out of the room, headed for the Gold Creek Saloon and a drink.

"So what could our fine Sheriff and these folks be talking about that's such a secret?" said Clay to himself as he poured another drink. Looking at the two gunmen he'd hired he had an idea. "I want you two to get out there and find out what the Sheriff is up to, but quietly. I don't want anyone in this town to think I'm involved," he said.

Quickly finishing their drinks, Red and Josiah grabbed their hats and headed towards the door. Turning back to Clay, Red asked, "Any place in particular you think we should start?"

"Try the Gold Creek, see if you can find one of the locals that might become talkative and buy him drink," said Clay, tossing a small bag of coins to the men. As the door closed behind them, Clay wondered what exactly the Sheriff and Bigsby had been talking about. It just wouldn't do for any attention to be focused his way right now.

Art hadn't said anything to his wife, Penny, but she could tell he was worried. Watching him as he busied himself behind the bar washing the same glasses for the third time, she knew it was time to try and get him to talk about it.

"Art, you've washed those glasses three times already, don't you think they're clean enough by now?"

Looking at her, Art realized he was indeed still washing the same batch of glasses. Shaking his head, he dried his hands and poured a shot from the special bottle under the bar.

"What is it Art?" asked Penny as she watched him hold the glass in his hand. "It's not like you to keep quiet when something's bothering you.

"It's that new fellow in town, Clay Francis," he answered. "Actually, it's what he's up to that bothers me. We've got ranchers, farmers and miners around here, and if it weren't for Stewarts' gang, very little trouble. So why do you suppose he's hired half a dozen gunslingers?"

"What makes you think they're gunslingers, Art?" asked Penny.

Art gave her an exasperated look as he lit a cigar. "I know they're gunslingers woman," he muttered. "Believe me, after a while you learn to recognize their type. I don't know what Mr. Francis is planning; but something that needs that many guns can't be good for Murieta."

"Then why don't you go to the Sheriff, let him know what you think," said Penny.

"Because right now all I have is a hunch, that's why." With that, Art grabbed the pan of water he'd been using to wash the glasses and headed for the back door.

Chapter 8

Bigsby, Handsome, Calaveras and Sheriff Martin were eating dinner at the jail when the door opened and John Lathrop walked in followed by a tall stranger they hadn't seen before.

"Howdy Sheriff," said John, nodding to the other three. "This here's a friend of mine, Tom Morris. We rode together a few years back and he looked me up yesterday since he was looking around out here to buy some land. He mentioned a gunman he ran across a few days ago, so after we buried those two that Bigsby shot, I asked him to come into town with me. I just dropped off their horses and gear at the livery. Bryce is writing up a receipt and said he'd drop it by later."

"Thanks John, I appreciate you taking the time to do this. Evening Tom. This is Bigsby, Handsome Longfellow and Calaveras." As the four men exchanged handshakes, Sheriff Martin asked John, "Did you find anything in their gear that points back to Stewart?"

"No, they had nothing like that on them, Sheriff. Just their guns, some tobacco and a couple of dollars were all they had between them." As he said this, John dropped a pair of gunbelts and a couple saddlebags on the desk.

"John, we could use your help, and we need to know where you stand, Tom," said Bigsby.

"Where I stand on what?" asked Tom. "I've only been in the area about a week. Came up on the train from San Francisco to Sacramento, and then started covering the land out here. I've been riding a horse for a lot of years, thinking of starting a ranch out this way."

"What do ya know about a fellow named Jesse Stewart?" asked the Sheriff.

"Nothing more than what John told me on the ride into town," replied Tom.

"So you know that Stewart runs a gang of outlaws around here that's been preying on the miners and ranchers, and has everyone afraid to testify against him," said Bigsby. "The Sheriff here tells me this gang operates out of some caves above Indian Diggings. They've got a lookout on the cliffs so it'd be pretty near impossible to get a posse in there unseen."

"Indian Diggings you say? Yeah, that's what he called that place." remarked Tom. "I rode through there a couple days ago. Ran into a rather unsavory fellow that suggested I look somewhere else for land. Since I wasn't interested in that particular spot I didn't see any reason to argue the point. He was wearin' a gunfighter rig that looked like it had seen a lot of use."

"I know the area you're talking about Sheriff," said John. Picking up a pencil from the Sheriff's desk he began sketching a map on the back of a wanted poster. "From what I saw of the place, if you try to come at 'em from the north, you'll be seen long before you get close; but there's a little slot canyon that comes in from the south west and ends about a quarter mile downstream from the mines. Most folks don't know about it, and they might not have anyone watching it."

"What's the bottom of the canyon like? Can we get horses through it?" asked Calaveras.

"It's only a couple of feet wide in places, no way to get a horse through. It wasn't made by a stream. Looks like the rock cracked during an earthquake. The bottom has a lot of rocks and branches in it, so we'll have to be careful moving through it" answered John.

"We?" asked Bigsby. "You sure you want in on this?

"You could wander around that area for days before you found it," said John. "From the main canyon all you can see is a pile of boulders, and from the upper end it's hidden in a thick patch of manzanita and digger pines."

"All right, so you show us where this little canyon of yours is located. Then what Sheriff? Stewart's supposed to have at least twenty men with him. There's only the five of use, which gives him a four to one advantage in guns." Handsome looked just a little bit uncomfortable as he said this.

"Trust Handsome to always be figuring the odds," said Calaveras. "But he does have a point."

"John, can we use this to get in behind the lookout?" asked Bigsby.

"It'll be a hard climb, but yeah, there's a spot we can use. It'll come out on Farnham Ridge south of Scott Creek. That should put you above and behind the gang's lookout," answered John.

"What's on your mind Bigsby?" asked Sheriff Martin.

"You put together a posse and get 'em ready about a mile or so from the hideout. John, Tom and I'll come up from behind and capture the lookout. Once we have them out of the way we'll signal you to bring in the posse quietly. We should be able to surprise his gang and capture them without anyone getting hurt," said Bigsby.

"Excuse me gentlemen, but aren't you forgetting someone? I failed to hear my name mentioned in this plan," said Handsome.

"Handsome, my friend," said Bigsby, "we do indeed have need of your talents. Here's what I want you to do." Bigsby pointed to the map John had drawn, and outlined what he wanted his friend to do.

"You want me to do what?" exclaimed Handsome, managing to look quite offended. "Not only is that unworthy of someone of my experience, but I refuse to even consider it!"

"Now Handsome, you're always telling us about your acting experience back east, so you should be well qualified for this," said Bigsby, clapping his friend on the shoulder. "We need to have the lookout busy while we climb out of that canyon. Once we have him captured, I'm counting on you to signal Sheriff Martin to bring in his posse. Of course, I could always mention to Art about that time in Fort Miller…."

"Alright, no need to mention that, I'll do it" whispered Handsome, looking quickly around. "But I'll remember this Bigsby!"

"I'm sure you will Handsome," smiled Bigsby at his friend. "Sheriff, Saturday morning before sun-up you have your men waiting here along Scott Creek. You won't be seen from there, and Handsome will be able to get to you quickly once we have the lookout taken care of."

"I should be able to round up a dozen men on the quiet and get 'em out of town without folks noticing," said Sheriff Martin. "We'll be ready when you give us the signal."

"Thanks Sheriff. Calaveras, John and I'll leave tonight and scout out the area," said Bigsby. "Handsome, you be ready at sunup Saturday. One of us will wave a red flag from the ridge, that's when you get the Sheriff and his men."

Chapter 9

Walking back to the livery with his friends, Bigsby told Handsome what he wanted him to do.

"With Calaveras and I dropping out of sight, we need you to be seen around town. Perhaps that way folks won't pay to much mind to what we might be up to."

"I'm sure that with very little effort Handsome can attract enough attention to himself that we won't be missed," offered Calaveras.

"I do believe I should be offended by that remark, Sir," said Handsome. "However, in the spirit of gentlemanly behavior, I'll ignore the insult and not take you to task this evening."

"I'm honored by your generosity Handsome," returned Calaveras.

"OK, you two finished?" asked Bigsby, laughing at his two friends.

"For the moment, yes," said Handsome as Calaveras just laughed and shook his head.

"We'll head over to my folks place, let them know what's happening, and then John will show us this area he's talking about." Bigsby was saddling his horse as he talked, taking care that the cinch was tight. Picking the bag of supplies off the hook next to the stalls, he divided the ammunition and food with John and Calaveras. Buckling the straps on his saddlebag, he then checked his Winchester in the scabbard and the ties on his bedroll. Satisfied, he turned to Handsome.

"You be careful," he said. "We don't know who Stewart has in town for spies, and we need you to be there Saturday morning."

"Haven't I always been there to cover you?" asked Handsome. "Well, ok, there was that time in Merced, but you know it was not my fault!"

"I know it wasn't. Just watch your back, and be ready for my signal."

Bigsby clasped his friend's hand in a firm grip, then turned and mounted his horse. John and Calaveras gave a wave as they turned and followed Bigsby out of town.

About an hour later John pulled up his horse and turned to Bigsby. "I'll be heading on up to the ranch from here, Bigsby. Need to let Angie know what we have planned. I'll probably stop at the O'Donahue place and see if they can help get the rest of the wood put up for her. You remember that spring we found about a days ride from your Pa's place?"

"The one under that lightning split pine? Yeah I remember that. Want us to meet you there?" asked Bigsby.

"That's right," said John. "I should be there by tomorrow afternoon. Give a whistle before you ride in so I know it's you."

"We'll be sure to do that. Tell Angie hello for us." Bigsby turned his horse onto the trail heading southeast as his friend rode out of sight.

"We should be at your ranch around midnight I reckon," said Calaveras as they walked their horses for a ways.

"That's what I figured," answered Bigsby. "We can rest a bit and feed and water the horses before we head out to meet John."

"You think this idea of yours is gonna work Bigsby?" asked Calaveras.

"I really do. If Stewart's gang is like most of them, they'll fall apart without a strong leader. Capture him, and I figure a lot of his men will cut and run. With Stewart in jail I think the folks in town will be less afraid and ready to help us round up the rest of them."

"You think the folks of Murieta will be ready for that?" Calaveras looked a bit skeptical.

"If we can capture Stewart, I'm sure of it." As Bigsby and his friend rode along, they continued to go over the plan, picking at it to see if there was anything they'd overlooked.

****

Ben Johnson had been a Deputy Sheriff less than six months and took his job seriously. He'd already walked Main Street to let folks know the law was around, and now he was walking the narrow alley behind the mercantile store. He was thinking of the apple pie his wife Mae had made that afternoon and how it was gonna taste with a cup of cold milk from the cellar, when a dark shape appeared out of the shadows in front of him.
"Can I help you?" he asked. He couldn't see the fellows face but thought it might be one of the new fellows he'd seen hanging around town this afternoon.

Starting to take a step back to give him room, Ben's arms were suddenly pinned from behind and a feed bag was pulled over his head. Struggling as hard as he could he almost had one arm free when something hard smashed into his skull, knocking him to the ground. Dazed from the blow, Ben had just started to get to his knees when a vicious kick drove the air from his lungs and left him gagging in the dust. An unseen hand grabbed his shirt, yanked him upright and slammed him into the rough boards of the buildings back wall.

"What were the Sheriff and his friends talking about in the Hotel today?" hissed a voice in Ben's ear.

"I don't have any idea," answered Ben, an answer which earned him a blow to the side of his head.

"Don't lie to me Deputy, it wouldn't be healthy," said his unseen attacker. "I want to know what they were talking about."

"I honestly don't know," replied Ben. "I wasn't even there. I haven't talked to the Sheriff since this morning."

"Well then, I strongly suggest you find out Deputy. We'll be in touch." A fist smashed into Ben's jaw and he dropped unconscious to the ground.

"Are you men really this monumentally stupid?" Red and Josiah spun around, hands drawing their Colts, to find Clay standing behind them, his anger clearly evident on his face. "I told you to find out without attracting a lot of attention. If the townspeople find out it was you two, then they'll know I was involved."

"We went to the saloon like you said, but no one was talking," said Josiah. Clay could tell by the man's attitude he had no idea why Clay was upset with him. "Only thing we was able to find out was that folks is too scared of Jesse Stewart and his gang to say anything."

"You told us to find out what the Sheriff was up to. We figured the Deputy would be sure to know," added Red. "Besides, we was careful, he won't have any idea who jumped him."

"You had better hope he doesn't, because if I have to change my plans because of your incompetence, I will shoot both of you myself!" Spinning on his heel, Clay stalked off, quickly disappearing in the darkness.

"Come on Josiah, grab his feet. We'll dump him behind the livery and leave a bottle of whiskey with him. Anyone finds him, they'll think he got drunk and passed out." Red was not at all happy at how Clay had yelled at them. Perhaps he'd have to 'discuss' it with him when this job was finished.

Chapter 10

When Bigsby and Calaveras rode up to his folks' place, the house was dark. Though it was about 10 o'clock, there was enough light from a half moon to see by as they walked their horses to the partially re-built barn. Dismounting they stripped saddles and blankets from their mounts and turned them into the corral. Bigsby forked some hay into a crib next to the fence while Calaveras poured a couple buckets of water into the trough. After seeing to the horses they picked up there gear and hung it on the posts set up along the wall of the barn.

"I see your Pa has been getting work done on the barn," remarked Calaveras as they started toward the house.

"Yeah, when I first got back here he was saying some men were going to be coming out to help him get the roof on. He figured he could get the rest done himself," said Bigsby.

"Mosebee, is that you?" Bigsby and Calaveras were surprised to hear Becca's voice coming from the house. Before they could answer the front door opened and she stepped out onto porch, a shawl wrapped around her shoulders, a lantern held high in her right hand.

"Ma, it's me, Bigsby, and Calaveras is with me. Is anything wrong? Where's Pa?" Bigsby and Calaveras quickly stepped up to the porch where Becca could see them.

"I don't know Bigsby, your Pa rode out of here this afternoon, said he needed to talk to Malcolm Snow about something. Said he'd be back by dark, and I shouldn't worry." She sounded angry, but in the glow of the lantern Bigsby could see the worry plain on her face.

"What's he need to talk to Malcolm about?" asked Bigsby. Most everyone in this part of the state knew Malcolm. An eccentric old man, he spent most of his time alone in a cabin near the spillway the miners had built on the Cosumnes River. A brilliant craftsman when it came to working with wood, he earned a living building and repairing anything from a wooden doll to the large freight wagons used to haul ore from the mines. He also seemed to know everything that was going on in the area, sometimes it seemed almost before the folks involved did.

"He wouldn't say." fretted Becca, "but I believe it had something to do with finding the men that attacked us. Mosebee hasn't talked about it much, but I know he intends to find those responsible."

"If your husband says he's going to find them, then you can be assured that he will." Calaveras had become good friends with Mosebee after helping his son bring home his bunch of cows.

"I know he'll find 'em. It's what'll happen when he does that scares me," said Becca.

Hearing a horse approaching them, the three turned and watched Mosebee ride up to the house. Quickly stepping down, Mosebee came over and grabbed Becca in a fierce hug.

"No need to worry about me, Becca. I can take care of myself." Putting her back down so she could get her shawl and nightgown straightened out he looked in her eyes. "Sorry I'm late. You know how old Malcolm can be. Took me a couple hours just to get him to stop talking about the armoire he's been commissioned to build for Mrs. Giles." Turning to look at his son and his friend, Mosebee gave them both a long look.

"You're going after Stewart aren't you?" he asked Bigsby.

"Yes Sir, we are. We've been talking to the Sheriff and we've got a plan."

"Well, go on inside then. Becca, put on some coffee will you? Let me take care of my horse and I'll be right along." He stepped off the porch and taking the reins, led his horse towards the corral.

"You heard him boys," said Becca. "Come on in and sit. I'll start the coffee and see if there's any of that cobbler I made yesterday left. If I don't put it away I swear that man would eat the whole thing at one sitting!"

Calaveras and Bigsby were sitting at the table finishing off the last of the cobbler when Mosebee returned to the house. Becca had just taken the fresh coffee off the stove and poured three cups as

Mosebee hung his hat on a peg by the door, then pulled out a chair and joined the two at the table.

"So you have a plan." He said.

"John Lathrop knows a way we can get a couple of men in behind the lookout at Stewart's hideout," explained Bigsby. "We take care of him and we can get Sheriff Martin and his posse up to the mine without alerting the gang."

"How're you going to get to the lookout without him hearing or seeing you coming?"

Smiling, Bigsby explained the role he'd asked Handsome to play in capturing Stewart and his gang. "We figure he'll distract the lookout enough that we can get close enough to knock him out without him raising the alarm. Then we signal Handsome and have him bring in the Sheriff and his posse."

"You know, I think that might just work. Any idea how many men the Sheriff will be able to get?" asked Mosebee.

"Don't know for sure, but he figured there were about a dozen he could count on. He's planning to go around to some of the ranches tomorrow and see how many men he can get from them. John Lathrop and his friend Tom Morris will meet us tomorrow, and then we'll head for that slot canyon John told us about," said Bigsby.

After talking for a few more minutes, Bigsby asked his Pa about Malcolm. "What were you trying to find out from old Malcolm?" he asked.

"I've been trying to find out who it was that attacked us that night, and I'd heard that Malcolm had some information that might be useful. I knew it was Stewart's men, but they had masks and I didn't recognize any of the horses." Mosebee took a sip of his coffee before continuing. "Malcolm said a couple of men came in to get a wagon wheel fixed, and he overheard them talking while he was working. He told me they were talking about the raid on our place and how this fellow was laughing about what happened to Becca."

"Did Malcolm know who they were?" asked Calaveras.

"No, but he said he heard them talking about the man that ordered the attack that night."

"It was Stewart, wasn't it?" Bigsby was sure that was the name Malcolm had over heard.

"No it wasn't," answered Mosebee. "Malcolm said the man they were talking about is called Sturgis."

"I've heard of him," said Calaveras. "Mean as a snake from what they tell me. Rider came through town a few weeks ago talkin' about a murder over near Sonora. Heard tell someone named Sturgis and two others beat a man to death over a card game. Said he was cheatin' them. When the Sheriff tried to arrest them they shot their way out of town, wounded the Sheriff and killed a young woman who had the bad luck to walk out of a store as they rode by."

"Did Malcolm give you a description of this guy, Pa?"

"Only that he wears a two gun rig tied down."

"Sounds like the one Tom Morris ran into, doesn't it Bigsby?" remarked Calaveras.

"Who's Tom Morris?" asked Mosebee.

"He's a friend of John Lathrop. They used to ride together. Anyway, he was scouting out the country, looking to settle down, and ran into this guy out near Indian Diggin's. Sounds like this Sturgis fellow."

"What're you going to do Pa?" asked Bigsby.

"Do? I'm going to find him, that's what."

"Mosebee, you can't. He might kill you!" cried Becca.

Getting up from his chair and putting his hand on Becca's shoulder, Mosebee said, "You know I'll be careful Becca, but I have to find him. We can't let men like him get away with attacking innocent folks and laughing at the law."

"Ma's right Pa. Can't you wait till we capture Stewart and his gang? Then Calaveras and I can go with you to get him." Looking at his Pa, Bigsby knew the answer even as he'd asked the question.

"You and Calaveras take care of Stewart. Maybe you'll even catch this Sturgis with them. In the meantime I'll look around town tomorrow, see what I can find out." Knowing his mind had been made up; Becca sat quietly and prayed her husband would come home alive after he found the man he was looking for.

Alright, Pa. Just be careful, that's all I can ask." Looking at his friend, Bigsby stood up. "Come on Bear, let's get some shut eye. We have a lot of riding to do tomorrow."

"Your right Bigsby, we do. Good night Mosebee, Ma'am," standing up, Calaveras shook hands with Mosebee and tipped his hat to Becca.

"We'll bed down out by the barn, Pa. Probably be gone by sunup tomorrow."

"Goodnight son, you and Calaveras be careful. Corner any living thing, man or animal, and it can get real mean." Becca stood on her toes to give her son a kiss, worry still clearly seen in her eyes.

"We will Ma, we will." Following his friend out he closed the door behind him.

The two men spread their blankets under the stars near the barn, checked their pistols and rifles and then lay down. Within minutes they were both asleep.

****

Leaving his folks place shortly after dawn, Bigsby and Calaveras headed up the narrow canyon of Dry Creek. The steep walls and rocky ground made for slow traveling, and several times they had to take to the stream bed to get around a pile of dead limbs or piles of boulders. About two hours after starting out they reached a rock slide that had partially dammed the creek, forming a large pond that filled the valley floor.

"That wasn't here before," said Bigsby as he searched the canyon walls for a way up.

"Don't remember it either," replied Calaveras. "We did have a lot of rain last winter; it might've come down then." Turning in his saddle Calaveras pointed out a faint game trail winding up the south wall. "Think we can get the horses up there?"

"Unless you want to back track about an hour I don't see any other way." Clicking his tongue, Bigsby urged his horse across the creek. Scrambling up the far bank the gelding momentarily lost it's footing before surging up the bank and onto the narrow trail. Calaveras' roan followed quickly, picking its way carefully through the rocks. Leaving the reins loose Bigsby allowed his horse to find the best footing as they moved forward.

When they reached the top of the ridge the horses were skittish and showing signs of being tired. Not wanting to be exposed on the ridgeline, Bigsby urged his horse forward into the trees before pulling it to a stop and dismounting. Calaveras joined him a minute later, taking a canteen from his saddle horn and offering it to Bigsby.

"Thanks, wasn't expecting the climb to be that hard." Taking off his hat Bigsby wiped his brow with his bandana. Grabbing his own canteen, he poured a little water into his hat and gave it to his horse. Calaveras did the same then looped the reins over a broken limb near the ground. Pulling a small telescope from a saddlebag, he pulled his rifle from its scabbard and walked to the edge of the trees where he could see out over the country to the south. The ridge was higher than those around it and offered a clear view towards the valley where Stewart was hiding his gang.

"How far away you think we are?" asked Bigsby as he crouched beside his friend.

"Probably not more than ten to fifteen miles if we had wings and could fly there," answered Calaveras. "Since we have to stay on the ground, probably more like twenty."

"You see anybody out there we need to worry about?"

"Nope, nothing but a few animals of the four footed kind," answered Calaveras. Shutting the telescope he got to his feet and offered a hand to Bigsby. "Let's get back on the trail; this detour's already cost us too much time."

"I know, it's going to be after dark before we get to where John and Tom will be waiting for us." Mounting up, Bigsby and Calaveras continued their ride up the valley to meet their friends.

****

That same morning Sally and Bryce were in their office next door to the livery doing paper work when there was a knock on the door and Handsome walked in.

"Morning Ma'am, Bryce," said Handsome as he removed his hat and walked forward to shake Bryce's hand. "I have a business proposition for you, concerning the procurement of the Meadowbrook Carriage you have stashed in the back of the stable. I'd like to rent it and I'm willing to pay the sum of twenty dollars."

Sally looked at Handsome, unsure if she should be impressed or insulted. "You're probably the only person between the Sierra's and San Francisco to recognize that carriage, and that means you also know what they're worth. So how can you have the nerve stand there and expect us to rent it to you for a mere twenty dollars?" The more she thought about it, the angrier she got. She'd inherited it from her Grandfather, who'd spent almost five hundred dollars to have it shipped here from back east. No way was she going to let this sissified rooster take it.

"Ma'am, I'm aware of it's' value, and believe me, if I didn't think the situation warranted, I would indeed be the last person to impose in such a fashion. If you and your husband would indulge me for just a few minutes, I'm sure I can explain." Handsome took a deep breath, reminding himself that when this was over, he was going to have a few words with Bigsby.

As he explained the plan Bigsby and the Sheriff had put together, he could see from their expressions that Sally and Bryce thought he was crazy. But as he answered their questions and explained the plan further, he could see they were about ready to go along. What he was a little worried about was the smile on Sally's face as he explained the other part of Bigsby's' plan.

"Handsome, that's about the most outrageous thing I've ever heard of!" Sally was laughing as she looked at Handsome and shook her head. "You men don't actually think this will work do you?"

Handsome was becoming very uncomfortable, but he had given his word, and as a gentleman, his honor demanded he follow through. "I realize it sounds very, unusual, Ma'am, but Bigsby does believe it will accomplish the task."

"I think he's right, Sally," said Bryce. "At least I think he's less likely to get shot on sight this way. And if it works, we can finally do something about Jesse Stewart and his gang."

"Oh, I grant you the element of surprise will be there alright," laughed Sally. Suddenly turning serious she looked at Handsome. "But if you get as much as a scratch on the Meadowbrook I will remove your hide, gentleman or not!"

"Believe me Ma'am; I will take the utmost care of it. It will be returned to you in the exact same condition as it is now." Handsome answered. "Now that we have reached an agreement on that matter, I would like to ask your assistance on that other part of Bigsbys plan."

"Come back tomorrow morning Handsome, we should have the carriage and everything else you asked for ready by then," said Sally.

"Thank you Ma'am, Bryce," said Handsome. Settling his hat back on his head he turned and walked out, closing the door behind him.

"Bryce, do you really think this crazy plan of theirs can work?" asked Sally.

"With Bigsby, Calaveras and Sheriff Martin involved? Yes, I think they might just pull it off. And crazy as it seems, Handsomes' part in the plan is what'll make it work." Bryce had to chuckle to himself as he pictured Handsome and his part in the plan.

"I'm really not that worried about the carriage, but I'm very worried about you being out there with the posse," Sally said. "You best not go out there and get yourself all shot up, you here me?"

"Don't worry Sally, I'll be careful. If they can get the lookout out of the way, I believe we can finally take care of Stewart's gang."

Chapter 11

Sheriff Martin was getting ready to ride out to the Eldritch place and see if he could get Matt and his sons, Todd and Jimmy to join the posse when the door to the office slammed open and little Tommy Jacobs barged in.

"Sheriff, come quick, he's dead, ya gotta see!" he yelled.

"Hold on Tommy, who's dead? Where?" asked the Sheriff as he grabbed his gunbelt off the peg by the door.

"Deputy Johnson, behind the livery, he's dead, I saw him, come on Sheriff, hurry!" Tommy was already running back out the door, not bothering to wait and see if the Sheriff was following.

As he stepped onto the street, he saw Art headed towards the Gold Creek Saloon.

"What's all the yelling about Sheriff? Young Tommy ran down the street like the devil was after him," said Art.

"Not sure Art, Tommy said he saw Ben Johnson dead behind the livery. Can you find Doc Barton and send him over while I check this out?"

"Sure thing Sheriff, I'll head over to his place now and bring him right along." Art turned and headed up the street while Sheriff Martin continued on to the livery.

Sally was coming out of the small house next to the livery when Sheriff Martin reached the short ally leading to the back of the building.

"What's going on Sheriff?" she asked.

"Young Tommy said he saw Ben dead behind the livery," said the Sheriff.

"Let me get Bryce and we'll be right there," said Sally as she headed back inside.

As he came around the corner, Sheriff Martin was relieved to see his Deputy sitting up and leaning against the corner of a crate Bryce had stored behind the livery. His eyes narrowed as he saw the empty whiskey bottle on the ground next to him.

"What happened here Ben?" he asked. Ben's jaw was swollen, and he was holding his side. It looked like he'd been in a fight.

"Two men jumped me behind the mercantile store last night when I was making my rounds, Sheriff." Ben was obviously still a little rattled from his experience.

"Did you get a look at them?" Martin asked.

"Naw, it was too dark to see their faces. One of them grabbed my arms while the other pulled a feed bag over my head. I almost got loose before someone hit me in the head and knocked me down. I think I got a broken rib when I was kicked in the side." From the careful way Ben was moving and breathing, Sheriff Martin figured he was probably right about the broken rib.

"Any idea why you got attacked Ben?" he asked.

"Yeah, they wanted to know what you and Bigsby was talking about at lunch yesterday," answered Ben. "When I told 'em I had no idea, they got mad, told me I better find out before they came back. Next thing I know I come to and hear Tommy yelling that I'm dead. Sure glad he was wrong Sheriff."

"So am I Ben. I was going to talk to you today about what's going on. Right now we need to have Doc Barton look you over; make sure they didn't bust that hard head of yours. You sure you don't know who they were?"

"Not positive, but from the way he moved, I think one of 'em was that new fella in town. He showed up yesterday, was hanging around Clay Francis's place."

"Yeah, I think I know who you mean. Look, I have to run out to the Eldritch place. Get yourself taken care of, let Mae know you're ok, then head over to the jail. As soon as I get back I'll meet you there and fill you in on what's going on." As he stood up,

Sheriff Martin turned to see Bryce, Sally and Art hurrying towards him.

"He's ok," he told them. "He just got beat up some. Sally, can you stay with him until Doc get's here?

"Sure thing Sheriff," answered Sally as she knelt beside the still wobbly deputy.

"Thanks. Art, can you and Bryce come with me?" Sheriff Martin was already headed for the front of the buildings.

As the three of them walked to front of the livery, Sheriff Martin filled them in on what Ben Johnson had told him.

"I have no idea what those men might be up to," he said. "I need you two to keep an eye out for them, and let me know where they are when I get back."

"Sure thing Sheriff, we can do that," said Bryce.

"Good, I'll talk to you both as soon as I get back." Striding towards his horse, the Sheriff quickly mounted and rode out of town.

Before they parted company, Art looked at Bryce. "I had a feeling there was something not square about that man," he said, clearly referring to Clay.

"I agree Art. Can't think of any other reason he'd be using force to try and find out what the Sheriff and Bigsby are doing," replied Bryce.

"Do you know what's going on?" Art asked.

"Nothing I can talk about right now, Art. You'll just need to wait till the Sheriff gets back."

"Well, alright, but you tell the Sheriff I don't appreciate being left out like this."

"I know Art, and I'm sorry. I think when you hear what the Sheriff has to say you'll understand."

Chapter 12

Phillips and Henderson were sitting on stools near the mine entrance drinking coffee when Bowden walked up. A tall lanky man from Mississippi, he had a quick temper and an equally quick gun hand.

"Get off your lazy asses and get saddled up," he told them.

Glaring back at him, Henderson tossed his coffee on the ground and slowly stood up. Phillips, moving only slightly faster, finished the last swallow from his cup, and then leaned over to put it in his saddlebag.

"Move, dammit, Stewart wants us to go over to the Eldritch place. Seems Mr. Eldritch hasn't sent his share in recently, and we're supposed to impress upon him the necessity of doing so."

"Okay, we're moving. Ain't nothin' to get excited about," said Phillips. "Ain't like Eldritch is gonna be moved out before we get there."

"Stop flappin' your mouth and mount up. Stewart's in a real bad mood today and you don't want to be any where around if he takes a mind to start shooting folks what bother him."

Remembering what happened to Stevens, shot in the back because Stewart thought he was arguing with him, Phillips and Henderson quit stalling and got their horses saddled quickly. Within five minutes of Bowden finding them they were on the trail, headed toward the Eldritch place.

****

Matt Eldritch had built his house next to Burgoyne Creek, protected from the southwest by a small rise, enough to block the worst of the winter rain storms. He was high enough above the creek to avoid the occasional flooding, but close enough that getting water to the garden and the stock wasn't too bad a chore. Live oak trees along the creek and on the ridge behind the house provided a supply of firewood and a bit of color when the summer dryness turned all the hills brown.

With the help of his two sons, Todd and Jimmy, Matt had the ranch working pretty well. He had about seventy-five head of cattle in the range to the north and a couple acres of vegetables. He occasionally sold a few head of cattle to the miners, along with some goats and chickens his wife Berta and daughter Megan raised. A blacksmith by trade, Matt did all his own shoeing and kept his plows, harnesses and wagons in good repair. Doing repairs and small jobs for some of the other ranches in the area also brought in a few dollars or perhaps a cow or goat in trade.

All in all, it was a pretty good life, he thought …at least it had been till the night Stewart's gang had attacked. Some of Stewart's men, wearing hoods, had ridden onto the ranch at night and set fire to the barn.

When Matt and his family had run out of the house to fight the fire, Stewart's men had caught them with ropes and forced them to stand helplessly by while it burned to the ground. Threatening to hang his wife and daughter in front of him if he didn't give them money, he'd had no choice but to give in to their demands.

Matt hadn't been thinking of that a few days ago as he'd walked out of his house to start his daily routine of chores. He'd been thinking of the horses that needed new shoes and the repairs he needed to make to the chicken coop.

Walking up to the new barn his neighbors had helped him raise after the other had burned, he'd almost walked past the open door before he'd noticed the paper stuck to the planks with the blade of the new ax head he'd been working on. Hands shaking, he'd pulled the blade out and unfolded the paper. Written in barely legible hand, it was a demand for more money, as well as a threat of what would happen to his family if he refused. Matt had crumpled the paper in his hand, shaking with rage. He'd shown the note to Berta after he'd gotten himself calmed down. That evening they'd told their sons about it, and as a family they'd decided there was no way in hell they were going to give in to Jesse Stewart and his bullies again.

This morning Matt had harnessed up the mules for some plowing and had left the yard as the sun came over the mountains.

"Whoa there mules," Matt called as he stopped them at the end of the row. Wiping the sweat from his face, he scanned the horizon as he'd been doing every few minutes for the last six days. He didn't see anything but the thin trace of smoke from the fireplace in the house. Satisfied, he turned to the plow and checked the Henry rifle in the scabbard strapped to the frame. Ever since he'd found the note on the door, he and his sons hadn't left the house unarmed. Todd and Jimmy were rounding up the cattle and moving them into the field below the house where the terrain there made a natural corral. He'd hold them there until he could move them into town. He'd promised to deliver thirty head to the miners, and he intended to keep his word. He knew Berta was keeping the shotgun close by while she and Megan did chores around the house and fed and watered the chickens and goats.

Walking over to the bucket he'd left under the small live oak, Matt picked up a dipper of water while once again scanning the surrounding land. A small cloud of dust was visible this time to the northeast where his sons had gone to collect the herd. Dropping the dipper, Matt kept his eyes glued to the cloud while he moved to plow and pulled his rifle from the worn scabbard. Smoothly levering a round into the Henry, he moved to the mules, ready to unhook the plow and run if he had to.

Dust and elbows flying, Todd and Jimmy rode their horses toward their father, whipping them hard in an effort to get them to run even faster. Matt unhooked the mules, turned one loose, and was mounted on the other when his boys rode up, pulling their mounts back onto their haunches to get them stopped.

"Pa, we got trouble", yelled Todd, his face pale. "Three men are headed towards the ranch from the east. One of 'em looks like that big fella that was with the gang that attacked us before."

"Get on to the house and get your Ma and sister inside. Todd, make sure there's water in the buckets. Jimmy, get the extra ammunition from the dresser in our room. I'll be right behind you," Matt told them.

As he rode the mule into the yard, he saw Todd carrying water buckets into the house while shutters were being closed from inside. Sliding off the mule, he ran for the front door, pulled it closed and slid the locking bar in place. Catching his breath, he looked around. Jimmy had the boxes of ammunition out on the table and was making sure the two pistols and extra rifle were loaded. Berta had the shotgun in hand and was putting extra shells into the pocket of her apron, and Megan was checking that all the window shutters were secured. Whatever else, he was proud of his family. They knew what needed to be done and saw to it.

"You think it's the same men that were here before, Matt?" Berta asked.

"Pretty sure they are, Berta. Todd said he recognized one of them."

"Pa, they're coming up the road from the creek," said Jimmy.

"All right, son. You go keep watch at the back of the house in case they try to get in that way. Holler loud if you see anything." Matt told him.

"Sure thing, Pa," answered Jimmy. "Megan, bring me that box of shells for the Winchester, will you?"

"As soon as I get this window shutter bar in place," his sister said.

"Todd, you're a better shot than I am. You take the new Winchester and watch the other window. Berta, you keep watch with the shotgun out that side window." Matt realized that with no windows on the south side of the house they were blind in that direction, but perhaps the blackberries over there would slow them down.

"Hey, Eldritch, come on out, we want to talk to ya," yelled Phillips. He was sitting on his horse about 20 yards from the front porch. As Matt watched, he stepped down and dropped the reins to his horse. He'd pushed back the muddy duster he wore and Matt could see the guns carried low and tied down. Off to the side he saw Henderson get off his horse, rifle in hand. "We came to collect the money you owe us. Pay up and we'll leave ya be!" The grin he couldn't hide told Matt he was lying.

"You can get the hell off my land, all of you," called Matt. "And tell your thieving boss Stewart we refuse to be bullied anymore."

"We thought you might try to act tough, Eldritch; but you ain't got the grit to take us on," taunted Phillips. Bowden was working his way around back, and Phillips needed to give him time to get in position.

"If you think that, why don't you come on up here and try and take our money," answered Eldritch. Big man like you with that fancy two-gun rig of yours ought to be able to take some money from us cowardly ranchers." Matt called back.

Henderson laughed at that, which made Phillips mad. "Shut your trap, Henderson," he snarled. "You think it's so damn funny, you go on up there and open that door."

"Not me," laughed Henderson. "This here's your shindig."

Watching from the back door of the house, Jimmy saw movement near the henhouse. Moving to the other side of the window, he was showered with glass as a rifle slug tore through the sash and buried itself in the wall. "Pa, there's someone out back," he yelled as he threw the rifle to his shoulder and fired.

Hearing the shots, Phillips pulled his .44's and fired twice at the house while running to get behind the Eldritch's wagon. Matt fired quickly but the slug from the Henry went wide. Henderson, finding himself the only target left, dropped the reins to his horse and took cover behind the water barrel near the corral. Shouldering his Winchester, he fired two shots at the window next to the front door.

"Is everybody ok?" yelled Matt. "Berta, are you all right?"

"I'm ok, Matt," she answered, as she dried her hands one at a time on her apron to get a better grip on the shotgun.

"I'm ok too, Pa," called Jimmy from the back of the house.

"You think they'll try to come in, Pa?" asked Todd. The nervousness was evident in his voice, but when Matt looked at him his hands were steady, his eyes concentrating on the yard where the gunmen were hiding.

"I don't know, Todd. We'll have to wait and see. Just be ready to shoot if the time comes. Jimmy, is anyone moving out back?"

"Not that I can see, Pa," Jimmy called back.

"Alright, keep a sharp eye out, they may try again."

"Never thought I'd have to shoot a man, Pa" Todd said. "Leastways not out here. Seemed like a good place till that gang moved in."

Berta was keeping watch out the side window while listening to her oldest son and husband talk. She was a practical woman, and living out here had taught her that sometimes you had to be hard to survive. She worried that her son might not live long enough to understand that himself. Just then a bush moved towards the back of the house. With no hesitation she fired and heard a muffled curse. Immediately she fired again at the bush, and then pulled back from the window to open the shotgun and get it reloaded.

"Todd, go see what's going on. I'll keep an eye out here."

"Ok, Pa. Be right back." Answered Todd as he moved to where his mother was watching through the window.

"Saw someone moving out by that patch of Scotch Broom," she said as Todd crouched down beside her. "I know I hit him, but I don't think he's hurt too bad."

"That accounts for the three of `em, Ma." said Todd. "Those two out front haven't moved since they shot at the house."

"Come on, Eldritch, throw out the money and your guns and we'll leave you alone!" yelled Phillips. Peering around the end of the wagon, he waved at Henderson. "Where's Bowden?" he asked.

"He was headed `round back," answered Henderson. "Heard a shotgun a minute ago. Don't know if he was hit."

"Damn. Now what do we do?" asked Phillips. This wasn't working out the way they'd planned. They sure hadn't expected Eldritch to grow a spine after what happened to his family the last time.

"You get around to the south side of the house and build a fire against the wall, then go watch the back door. We can get `em all when they try to escape!"

"They got a woman and a girl in there, Phillips. I ain't gonna have no part in burnin' women or children," Henderson called back in disbelief. He looked at Phillips and found himself looking down the bore of Phillips' rifle.

"You'll do it ya yella coward, or by God I'll shoot you right now," snarled Phillips. "I'll keep their heads down while you make a break for the trees. From there you can make it around to the side."

Henderson stared at Philips for several seconds before he finally nodded. He might get shot before he got to the trees, but he was definitely dead if he didn't do what Phillips wanted.

"Get ready," Phillips called, then stood up and started levering his rifle as fast as he could, aiming for the windows in the front of the house.

"Get down," hollered Matt as he jerked back from the window. The logs gave plenty of protection from the slugs hammering into the house, but there was still plenty of danger from the flying glass or a stray bullet as the windows shattered. Matt just caught a glimpse of Henderson as he ran for the trees. He and Todd both fired a shot but missed as Henderson ducked under the branches of the live oaks.

Sheriff Martin pulled his horse to an abrupt stop as he heard the rifle fire erupt. It had to be coming from the Eldritch's place on the other side of the low ridge. Grabbing his rifle, he dismounted and dropped the reins to his horse. Crouching as low as he could, he hurriedly made his way to where he could see down into the Eldritch place. Using a low bush to hide his outline, he searched the scene below for the source of the gunfire. Spotting movement by the wagon, Martin waited and recognized Phillips when he rose up to shoot at the house again. He heard the report of two more rifles as Todd and Matt returned fire.

Seeing two strange horses in the yard, he looked around again. Looking towards the back of the house, Martin spotted Henderson moving towards the south side of the house through the small stand of live oak. Knowing the house had no windows on that side,

Martin decided to go after Henderson. It looked like the Eldritch's had Phillips pinned for now.

Moving quietly, Martin ducked back below the ridge and then turned and ran to where a clump of blackberry bushes grew down towards the house. Keeping low as he crossed the ridge, he followed the bushes towards the back corner of the house. When he looked, he could see Henderson squatting next to the base of the wall, his body hiding his actions. When he saw the curl of smoke over Henderson's shoulder, he realized they were trying to burn them out. Martin quietly moved towards Henderson, gun drawn. When he was about ten yards away, he stopped.

"Freeze, Henderson," he barked. "Put your hands high, then stand up slowly and turn around."

Henderson raised his hands and stood, but as he turned he threw the small knife he'd palmed at Martin's face while grabbing for his gun and firing. Dodging to his left, Martin felt the bullet slap at his shirt sleeve as his own gun thundered twice. Through the smoke he saw Henderson stagger backwards against the house and then fall into the pile of brush he'd set to burn against the house.

Martin quickly pulled Henderson to the side and stomped out the flames. After checking to make sure that the outlaw was dead, he moved towards the front of the house.

When he looked out into the yard, Martin could see that Phillips was still hiding behind the wagon. At the same time he heard the sounds of a running horse. Turning to look over his shoulder, he caught a glimpse of a rider, bent low over his horse, high-tailing it out.

"Looks like your friends are either dead or have run out on you, Phillips. Might as well make it easy on everyone and give up," called Martin.

"That you Sheriff Martin?" asked Phillips.

"That's right, Phillips. Throw down your guns and no one else has to get hurt."

"I go back with you, Sheriff, and they're gonna hang me," said Phillips.

"Probably so. You got a lot to answer for. But I give you my word you'll get a fair trial."

"Your word," spat Phillips. "What makes you think I'd take the word of a lousy lawman, Sheriff?" Phillips edged towards the end of the wagon. His horse was just a few yards away. If he could convince the Sheriff he was giving up, he might have a chance to get away. "Tell you what, Sheriff; come out where I can see your face. Maybe then I might believe you."

"I'm not a fool, Phillips. Throw out your guns. Then we'll talk."

"All right damn you….here." Phillips stood up and threw his rifle out into the yard. As soon as he did, he turned and ran for his horse. Jumping into the saddle, he pulled his Colt and started shooting towards the Sheriff as he spurred his horse. He hadn't made twenty feet when Matt shot him out of the saddle.

When Sheriff Martin reached him, Phillips was still alive. Turning him over, Martin saw the huge wound in his chest and knew he wouldn't last long.

"How many men does Stewart have, Phillips?" he asked the dying man.

"More `n you got, Sheriff," gasped Phillips. He coughed once, shuddered briefly and died, his body going limp in the Sheriff's hands.

Letting the body fall back on the ground, Martin stood up and turned to meet Matt and Todd coming across the yard.

"He dead, Sheriff?" asked Matt.

"Yeah, he is. So's his buddy Henderson, out beside the house. I caught him trying to set fire to your place. Shot him when he drew down on me."

"I think there's another one around, Sheriff. Jimmy and Berta both got a shot off at someone besides these two," said Matt. "Berta thinks she might have hit him with the shotgun."

"That must've been the fellow I saw hightailing it outta here then," said Martin. "From what I saw of him, he might've been injured. But he's a long way from here by now I reckon."

"Well, we're mighty glad you showed up when you did, Sheriff. But why did you show up today? You got something on your mind?"

"Matter of fact I do, Matt, and it concerns what just happened here. Let's get these bodies into the wagon, and then I'd like to talk to you and your family. When I'm done, I'd like you to take them to the undertaker in town. They don't deserve it, but they'll get a decent burial."

"All right, Sheriff, I'll listen. Todd, you and Jimmy round up their horses and tie `em to the back of the wagon. Sheriff, you grab his feet and we'll start loading this one. Berta, would you get that piece of canvas by the feed sacks in the barn?" Matt was anxious to get this done and find out what the Sheriff wanted.

Half an hour later Matt and his sons were sitting at the table with Sheriff Martin. Berta had brewed a pot of coffee and brought it to them with some cups. As she started to pour the coffee, Martin took the pot from her and asked her to have a seat.

"This concerns you as well, Berta, so I'd like you to listen as well." Turning to Matt, he began to explain what he had in mind. "As you probably already know, those two dead men out there ran with Jesse Stewart's gang. I know what he did to you and your family, Matt. The same things have been happening all over this area. Problem is, they have folks scared and no one is willing to testify against them." Sheriff Martin walked to the window then turned around and faced the Eldritch family again.

"About a week ago, Bigsby got back into town after he found out about the attack on his parents. Since then he's been attacked twice by Stewart's men, and both times they were talking about a bounty on Bigsby's head." Martin took a sip of his coffee before setting the cup down. "With that information," he continued, "we have enough to go after Stewart and his gang for attempted murder."

"You're planning to take on his gang, Sheriff?" Matt looked a little stunned at what he'd just heard.

"Yes, Matt, we are," the Sheriff replied. "Bigsby, along with Calaveras Bear, Handsome, John Lathrop, Tom Morris and I, have come up with a plan we think will work. John knows a way we can get close enough to take care of his lookouts without being spotted. Once they do that, we can get a posse close enough to capture them. We believe that once they realize they're trapped in the mine, they'll surrender. I came out here to ask if you'd join us, Matt."

Berta's hand flew to her lips as she inhaled sharply. Matt looked at Sheriff Martin for a moment, then turned to his wife and took her hand.

"You know this is something I have to do," he said softly. When she started to shake her head no, he gently held it in both hands. "You remember what they did to you and Megan when they were here before, and you know they weren't going to just let us go this time, don't you?" When she nodded, Matt turned and spoke to Sheriff Martin again. "Todd and I will join you, Sheriff. What is it you want us to do?"

"Pa, what about me?" asked Jimmy.

"I need you to stay here and look after your Ma and sister, Jimmy. I'm counting on you to do that."

"All right, Pa. I'll do as you say." Jimmy was clearly not happy to be left behind, but he'd do as his Pa asked.

"Matt, tomorrow night at about two hours after dark I want you and Todd to meet us about eight miles south of town along the Jackson Road. We'll be riding hard so make sure you've got good strong mounts, and bring plenty of ammunition. We hope they'll surrender, but they may decide to fight."

"Okay, Sheriff. We'll be there," said Matt. "Jimmy, get the team hitched to the wagon, would you? Then you and I'll drive the bodies into town for the Sheriff. Berta, would you get together a list of supplies I can get at Fiddletown's? No sense in wasting a trip."

Chapter 13

Two miles from the Eldritch place, Bowden stopped his horse in a small thicket of young poplars where he could see his back trail. His arm was hurtin' something fierce from the buckshot. Damn, he hadn't been expectin' that! He also knew he could lose the arm if he didn't get it out.

After watching for several minutes, he was satisfied there was no immediate pursuit. Carefully dismounting he walked over to the small stream running through the thicket. He pulled his knife out as he knelt down and used it to cut away the sleeve of his shirt. Dipping the cloth in the stream he began to wash away the dirt and blood on his arm, cursing loudly at the pain that lanced through it to his shoulder. Luckily it wasn't his shooting arm. Jesse Stewart had no use for a man what couldn't hold a gun. Wiping his knife on his pants leg, Bowden gritted his teeth and began to dig at the first of the many holes the buckshot had punched in his upper arm.

Almost an hour later, still cursing, only louder and meaner, Bowden staggered back to his horse. Grabbing the bottle of whiskey he had stashed in his saddlebag, he yanked out the cork with his teeth and spat it out on the ground. Tipping his head back, he took several long swallows before lowering the bottle.

Wiping his mouth with the sleeve on his good arm, he poured some over his wounds. The fresh pain caused by the burning of the alcohol started him off on another string of curses. Stopping to catch his breath, he looked at the whiskey remaining in the bottle, then tipped up the bottle and finished it off. Throwing the empty bottle into the brush, he stripped off his kerchief and tied it around his arm.

Figuring he'd done all he could, Bowden grabbed the reins to his horse and after several tries, was able to haul himself into the saddle. It was a good two or three hours to the hideout, but he figured the whiskey would dull the pain for a while. Stewart was going to be furious that two men were dead and he didn't get any money, so mad in fact he'd probably shoot him before he had a chance to tell him about the Sheriff.

Checking the rough dressing one last time, Bowden settled his hat on his head and squared himself in the saddle. Yanking the horse's head around, he pointed him towards the hideout and started off at an uneven trot.

****

"Mr. Standeford, I wonder if I might have word with you." The smooth voice with its hint of a Southern drawl broke through Bryce's concentration on the wheel spoke he was shaping for the Morgan's wagon. Keeping his face blank, he turned to face the man standing at the open door of the livery barn.

"What can I do for you, Clay?" he asked, wiping his hands on a bit of rag he kept on his bench.

"I thought perhaps you might know where I can find our Sheriff this afternoon? I've asked around and no one seems to have seen him. I find that rather strange, don't you?" Clay moved closer to Bryce as he talked, his spurs making a small silvery sound as he approached.

"I don't think that's strange at all," said Bryce. "The Sheriff has a job to do, and sometimes he's not around for a day or so."

""So you have no idea where he might be right now?" To Bryce, Clay seemed almost anxious for his answer.

"Right now? No I don't. I saw him this morning when they found Ben Johnson, and he mentioned he had business with Matt Eldritch. I assume that's where he went, but couldn't say for sure."

"Yes, terrible business that. About the Deputy I mean. Makes you wonder if we have the right man in place as Sheriff, with folks getting attacked right here in town. It's shameful." In spite of his words, Bryce was sure the safety of the town wasn't high on Clay's list of concerns.

"Why are you looking for the Sheriff, Clay?" asked Bryce.

"I understand that this Stewart and his gang have been attacking people around this area for some time. Naturally, as a property owner I'm concerned about what's being done to apprehend this criminal." When he finished talking, Clay took a small cigar from his vest pocket. Taking a match from a can nailed to the post by the oil lantern, he lit the cigar then dropped the match and ground it into the dirt floor with his boot. "I simply wanted to offer my assistance to the Sheriff, in any way I might be able to help."

"Why would you offer to do that, Clay?" Bryce didn't like what he'd heard about the man. He believed in dealing square with people, and had no regard for those that didn't. "From what I hear, that's about the last thing I'd expect from you."

"Now why would you say that, Bryce? I have a vested interest in what happens in this town. The fact that one of its citizens is being threatened affects me as much as anyone else."

"Like the interest you showed in Gary Haling?" asked Bryce. "We heard what happened to him when he didn't want to sell out to you."

"I have no idea what you're talking about. I offered him a fair price and he took it. I understand he was going to buy some land up in Oregon."

"Thing is, he hasn't been seen since. Tom Trobien came through here a couple days ago; said most of Gary's stuff was still at his cabin. Now why would a man about to move to Oregon leave all his stuff behind like that?"

"Perhaps he intended to buy what he needed when he got up there," answered Clay. He was beginning to wonder about the story Red had told him about Haling. "If he was in a hurry to get there, it might have seemed an acceptable trade to him. In any case, I must be on my way. I have business at the bank. If you see the Sheriff, would you please inform him of my offer?"

"Yeah, sure, I'll do that." Bryce knew he was being rude, but just couldn't help himself.

****

The shadows were beginning to slide towards late afternoon when Clay rode into the rough camp Josiah and Red had setup next to a small creek. Located on a small patch of ground where the stream looped away from the rock wall, it was hidden from passers-by but offered a view of the road into town. As he stepped from the saddle of his bay, Clay was working hard to keep his anger in check.

"Well look here, Josiah. Seems Mr. Clay Francis's decided to pay us a visit." Red had been drinking most of the afternoon, and the liquor had done nothing to improve his mood. "Sorry we can't offer you a chair, but since you run us out of town, we haven't had the pleasure of the nicer things."

"You know very well I didn't 'run you out of town' as you so crudely put it," said Clay. "After what you did to the deputy, I needed you two to remain unseen for a time. It was your choice to move out here."

"Our choice? And just where in the hell were we supposed to stay in town?" Red answered back. "You didn't want us at your place, and there ain't but one hotel in town, in case you missed that bit of information." He was drunk and he was mad. Clay had embarrassed him in front of Josiah, and he was looking to get even.

"You made the choice so stop sniveling and deal with it. For now, I want to know what really happened with Haling." Clay was close to losing his temper and found himself regretting he'd ever hired Red Peters.

"Nothing happened. We gave him the money, he made his mark on the deed, and then he left." The guilty look on Red's face told Clay what he needed to know.

"I don't believe he really left, now did he, Red?" asked Clay with the anger evident in his voice.

"What do you care, you got the deed you wanted."

"What I wanted was to get the deed in a way that couldn't be challenged in court you idiot!" In spite of himself, Clay found he was shouting. Struggling to get himself back under control, he quietly asked, "What happened to the money you were supposed to pay Haling for the deed, Red?"

Cursing, Red charged to his feet, fingers curled near the grip of pistol.

"You callin' me a thief now, Clay? First you come in here and accuse me of lying, and now you call me a thief? No man does that to me!" The words were barely out of Red's mouth when he grabbed his pistol and fired. He barely had time to register that he'd missed before Clay fired, hitting Red square in the forehead.

As the outlaw dropped dead to the ground, Clay swung his Remington to cover Josiah before the other had his pistol clear. Moving slowly, Josiah dropped the Colt back in his holster and slowly raised his hands.

"What're you planning to do now, Clay?" he asked.

"Did you and Red kill Haling?"

"Yeah, what of it? You were willing to pay that money to get his deed and we got it for ya. Why do you care who ended up with the money?"

"It's very simple. The last thing I need is for people to be asking questions; and, because of you two, people are starting to ask questions."

As he finished talking Clay calmly pulled the trigger and shot Josiah through the heart. Putting his pistol away, he began searching through the pairs' meager belongings, quickly finding what was left of the cash he'd given them to pay off Haling. Stashing it in his saddle bags, he found a small shovel in their pack and began scooping out a hollow in the soft ground.

Two hours later Clay had buried the two men and hidden their gear in a hollow behind some fallen boulders. Turning their horses loose, he figured the camp was secluded enough that it might remain undetected for a long time; long enough to be finished with his plans for buying land around Murieta.

Chapter 14

By the time Bowden got back to the hideout the fierce pain in his arm had pretty well sobered him up. Waving the signal to the lookout, he turned his horse up the trail to the mine. Stewart and Del Rogers watched from the porch of the mine shack while he stripped the saddle and blanket from his horse and turned it into the corral. Nobody said a word as he struggled one-armed with the weight of the saddle before finally getting it across the top rail of the fence. Turning to see if there was any coffee in the pot the cook always kept by the fire, he staggered back as he came face to face with Stewart.

"So where's the money Bowden?" asked Stewart. "And where's Henderson and Phillips?"

"We didn't get any money, Jesse. Someone musta tipped them off we was coming. By the time we got to the house they was holed up inside." It wasn't the complete truth, but Bowden knew Jesse was likely to kill anyone he thought was unfit for the job. "We spread out and was surroundin' the house when they started shootin'. I caught a load of buckshot in the arm, and Phillips got pinned down in the front yard. Henderson managed to get to the side of the house and was startin' a fire to burn em out when the Sheriff rode up and started shooting."

"Sheriff Martin, what the hell was he doing there?" Stewart was clearly surprised by this bit of news. "I thought we had him runnin' scared."

"I don't know why he was there, Jesse. He bushwhacked Henderson, shot him dead while he was startin' the fire, then he and Eldritch fooled Phillips into surrenderin' and shot him down like a dog when he did. I managed to get away and got back here soon's I could." Bowden had no idea if Phillips was really dead or not, but it sounded like a good story.

"Damn it, we can't have that tin star going around stirring folks up, if that's what he's doing. Del, take the kid and get into town, see if you can find out what the Sheriff was doing at the Eldritch place. Bowden, have Cletus take a look at that arm. And you'd best not be lying to me, or I'll stake you out and gut you like a deer." Turning on his heel Stewart stalked back into the mine shack, slamming the door with a bang that echoed off the canyon walls.

Looking at Bowden, Del slowly shook his head. "Jesse does get mighty mad when something doesn't go the way he planned it. He's gonna be a pure bother till we can get things back the way he likes it. Come on, let's find the kid and get Cletus to fix you up." Together the two men walked towards the mine entrance, listening to the curses coming from the shack.

****

Standing in the shadows outside the Gold Creek Saloon, Sturgis watched the quiet street. He'd been keeping an eye on the town for Stewart, and knew when Bigsby had arrived. He'd seen him meet with Handsome, kill Max Teague, then join Calaveras and the Sheriff at the hotel. He figured Bigsby was going to be foolish and try to find out who'd been responsible for the attack on his folks, and was actually looking forward to killing him when the time came. He'd heard the stories that Bigsby was good with a gun, but he knew he was faster.

Seeing them get together later at the Sheriff's office with Lathrop and the stranger he'd chased away from the gang's hideout, he'd sent a message up to Stewart. Since then, Handsome was the only one still around. Even Sheriff Martin had been gone all day. Something was going on, but he hadn't gotten close enough to find out what it was.

Finishing his smoke and flicking the remains into the street, he decided he needed a drink. Pushing through the swinging doors, he spotted Doc Barton at a table by himself. Interesting, he thought. You didn't see the Doc in here very often.

Sitting at the table with the bottle in front of him, Doc couldn't for the life of him figure out why he'd agreed to go with the posse. He'd gotten so worked up over it, he'd decided to come down to the saloon for a drink "to relax himself". He was about a third of the way through the bottle when he heard someone pull out a chair at his table and sit down.

"Hate to see a fella drinkin' by hisself," said Sturgis as he reached into his pocket. Pulling tobacco and papers from his pocket he rolled a cigarette, scratched a match into flame on the table, and lit up while watching Doc Barton through the smoke. Perhaps the reason Doc was getting himself thoroughly drunk would be interesting to hear.

"Yeah, I hate it too," slurred Doc. "Why doncha' get a glass 'n join me?" he asked.

"Don't mind if I do." Sturgis waved at the bartender who tossed him glass from behind the bar. "Man sitting here drinking alone, I figure it has to be either woman or money trouble."

"Nah, it ain't either one a those," answered Doc as he reached for the bottle and tried to pour himself another drink.

Taking the bottle from him, Sturgis picked up the glass Doc had knocked over and poured it full of whiskey. He slid the glass in front of Doc as he said, "Doc, you ain't a drinkin' man, so for you sit here like this something's really got to be eatin' at ya."

"Not 'sposed to talk about it, can you believe that?" said Doc. "I'm a gentleman, a medical doctor, not some uncivilized roughneck. What on earth do I know about firearms, horses, or arresting outlaws?"

Now this is interesting, thought Sturgis. I need to find out just what has Doc Barton this upset. "You're right Doc, what has that sort of thing got to do with you? Stitching folks up, delivering babies, giving Miss Ida something for her vapors, that's what you do for this town."

"You're correct Sir. I do this town a great service, and I do it right here in town. I have no call climbing on a horse and traveling the country." Doc was gratified to find someone who understood the unfair burden that the Sheriff had placed on him.

"Traveling the country? Unless you had to make a call to one of the homesteaders to deliver a baby, why would you need to leave town?" asked Sturgis.

"Sheriff Martin told me I couldn't talk about it to anyone," said Doc. "He said there were um, uh, spies in town, and we had to keep our plans a secret." Doc was getting to the point where he was barely able to stay in his chair. "If Jesse Stewart found out there'd be trouble."

"Spies? What spies?" asked Sturgis, chuckling to himself.

"Sheriff Martin said if Jesse Stewart knew the posse's plans he might get away," said Doc. "He said if he knew the posse was coming for them in two days, he might ambush them, or run away, or something like that."

For the moment Sturgis could only sit and stare at Doc Barton. The Sheriff was actually going to try and take Stewart? He needed to get word to the hideout as soon as possible!

"Doc, you must've had too much to drink. The sheriff would never try to take on Stewart, why, his gang would tear this town apart!"

"Nope, they got a plan, gonna sneak up on him." Doc said, trying to focus on the glass he was holding. "We're supposed to meet out on the Jackson

Road at midnight day after tomorrow." Doc had a vague thought that perhaps he shouldn't be saying this, but he was too drunk to care.

Day after tomorrow, thought Sturgis. That was plenty of time to get the boys together and plan a little surprise for the Sheriff and his posse.

"The Sheriff can't make you do something you don't want to do, Doc," said Sturgis. "If I were you, I'd go home and get a good nights sleep and go about my business like nothing happened."

"You, you're quite right Sir, I think I'll do just that!" Having said that, Doc stood slowly up from his chair, tugged his vest down, and staggered out the door.

"Stupid drunk," thought Sturgis, watching him leave. "He has no idea he just gave Stewart the whole plan. When I get there tomorrow, we'll have plenty of time to get ready for the Sheriff and his posse!" Getting to his feet, Sturgis headed out the back door of the Gold Creek, nodding to Nelson as he passed. Nelson finished his drink and then got to his feet and followed Sturgis.

Just outside the door to the saloon Sturgis turned to Nelson. "That drunken old fool just told me the Sheriff is putting together a posse to go after Stewart. I'm headin' up to the hideout to let him know so we can plan an ambush for the Sheriff and his posse. I want you to follow the Doc home and take care of him."

"You want me to kill the Doc? Why, he ain't any threat to us."

"Because he might remember what he told me tonight and then tell the Sheriff you idiot," growled Sturgis. "Now get going and get rid of that old fool before he can cause us any trouble." Shoving Nelson away from him Sturgis turned and headed down the alley towards his horse.

****

"Where are you going in such a hurry Sturgis?" The words coming out of the dark stopped Sturgis cold, afraid to make any move at all for the .44's strapped to his legs.

"Who's there?" he called. "You got a quarrel with me, show yourself! Or are you too yellow to face me square?" He'd ambushed enough men in his past to know not to expect any mercy. His only hope was to try and stall enough to figure out where his attacker was hiding.

"I'm a lot braver than you were you son of a bitch," said Mosebee, stepping out of the shadows to face Sturgis in the alley. "You sent the men that raided our place that night. You're the one responsible for Becca's leg, and the nightmares she has of masked riders burning our home and riding her down,"

"Mosebee?" asked Sturgis. "What the hell are you talking about? I had nothing to do with that. I got witnesses that'll swear I was in the Gold Creek that night."

"I know you weren't there that night," said Mosebee. "But you gave the orders, you sent those men to destroy our ranch and drive us out because we wouldn't give in to Stewart's threats."

"You got no proof I had anything to do with that."

"I have all the proof I need. Folks have been murdered, robbed, and beaten by men sent out by you and Stewart. Well, that's going to stop, beginning with you. You're going to die tonight, Sturgis."

"Then draw dammit," hissed Sturgis as his hands flashed to his guns. Before he could even clear leather he saw the flame from Mosebee's gun and felt the bullet smash into his chest.

Looking down at the body of Sturgis, Mosebee slipped his Colt back into its holster. "That's one less outlaw for you to worry about, Sheriff."

****

Doc Barton was talking to himself as he stumbled along the street towards his office. He lived in a small apartment behind his examination room, with a door opening onto the alley between buildings.

"I never drink more than a glass of brandy once a month, so why did I drink all that whiskey?" Barely able to stand, he fumbled with the door before getting it open. Staggering across the room he fell onto his bed without bothering to take off even his hat. Within seconds the sound of his snoring began to fill the room, covering the sound of the hinges as the door slowly swung open.

Standing in the door to the Doc's apartment, Nelson looked back up the alley before quickly stepping inside and closing the door. It was black as pitch inside, but with the noise the Doc was making, he didn't need any light.

Moving to the bed, he carefully felt around and determined that Doc was actually lying across the bed. Moving his hands slowly, he determined where Doc's head was, then picked up a pillow and holding it in both hands put one knee in Doc's back and pushed the pillow down hard over the mans head. Doc began to struggle as his lungs starved for air, arms and legs flailing wildly. Nelson leaned more weight onto the helpless mans body until finally his struggles waned and then stopped all together. Remaining in position a little longer, Nelson then stood up and dropped the pillow on the floor beside Doc's body. Turning quickly, he retraced his steps to the door, and after checking the alley again, closed it behind him and walked quickly towards the hotel.

As he stepped out into the street in front of the hotel, Nelson heard a shot echo from behind the saloon. Pulling his gun he crept up to the corner of the building and looked into the alley. From the light coming through a window he saw Mosebee standing over Sturgis' body. Heart pounding, Nelson quickly holstered his pistol and moved back before he was seen. Running quickly to the street, he jumped on his horse and whipped it into a gallop towards Jackson Road, a cloud of dust following as he raced for the trail to Indian Diggings.

****

Sheriff Martin was in his office when the door opened and Mosebee walked in. Putting down the stack of wanted posters he'd received from Sacramento, he looked on as Mosebee walked over and dropped a gunbelt with two Colts still in their holsters on the desk.

"What's all this then?" he asked Mosebee. Without looking at the gunbelt he tipped back in his chair and looked at the man standing before him. He considered Mosebee a friend and knew how much it had hurt him, what had been done to Becca. He'd expected sooner or later he was going to have to deal with this.

"Belonged to a snake name of Sturgis," said Mosebee. "He's dead, and I shot him."

"Was it a fair fight? Maybe self-defense?" asked Martin.

"No, not really. I found out he was the one ordered the attack on my place. When I confronted him tonight he didn't deny it, tried to draw on me. I already had my gun out and shot him down." Taking off his own gunbelt, Mosebee dropped it alongside the outlaws rig. "Guess you better arrest me, Sheriff. I figure the judge might not take too harsh a view of me, considering what they did to Becca."

Sheriff Martin looked at his friend for a moment, noting there was no pleasure in his eyes for what he'd done, just a look that said he done what he felt he had to do.

"Well, Mosebee, actually I don't have to arrest you." Reaching for the stack of posters, he thumbed through them, found the one he wanted, and flipped it onto the desk. "This came in from the office in Sacramento today. Seems there's a bounty on that fellow you shot, and it's dead or alive. He shot several people down in Sonora, killing a young woman while getting away. I'll send a telegram to the Sheriff in Sonora and tell him Sturgis is dead. Put your gun back on and get out of here."

"Well I'll be, Sheriff." Mosebee shook his head, and then placed the poster back on the desk. "Two hundred dollars, that's a lot of money, even for a murderer."

"Guess the young lady he killed was the daughter of a rich man in Sonora. He's the one put up the reward."

"Alright, Sheriff, I'll take the money. I can use it to help finish rebuilding the barn and getting some more cattle to replace the ones we lost in the raid." Picking his gunbelt up, Mosebee buckled it around his waist. Nodding at the Sheriff he turned and walked out of the office.

Watching him leave, Sheriff Martin found himself wishing he'd asked Mosebee to be on the posse, but he hadn't. If they didn't catch Stewart in the raid, chances were real good he'd retaliate by hitting their place again.

Chapter 15

When Bigsby and Calaveras finally reached the split tree it was after dark. Calaveras whistled softly as they approached. Hearing an answering whistle from the shadows under the tree, they moved forward. John and Tom had a small smokeless fire going behind the downed trunk of a tree, a pot of coffee perched on the rocks beside the pit.

"What took you so long boys? Calaveras, this green horn get you lost again?"

"No, he did fine, John. Rock slide blocked the valley above his folk's place, so we had to climb out and travel along the ridge for a while. That probably cost us three or four hours. Brush has really grown up in the last couple of years, slowed us down a bit." As he was talking, Calaveras and Bigsby pulled their saddles off their horses. While Bigsby stacked their gear along the log sheltering the fire, Calaveras took the horses down to the stream to drink.

"We got a good look at the country from the ridge. Didn't see anybody moving around," said Bigsby as hepicked up the coffee pot and poured a cup. Sitting down, he looked at his friends, being careful to keep his gaze away from the flames. Experience had taught him that if you looked into the fire, it'd take several seconds for your eyes to adjust enough to see anything coming in from the darkness.

"Neither did we," said Tom. "We thought we might have heard some shots over to the west earlier this afternoon, but wasn't sure."

"Pa found out who ordered the attack on his farm. Said it was a fellow named Sturgis, wore two guns tied low. Sounded like that fellow you ran into, Tom."

"Yup, that might have been him. I didn't like the look of him at all. He had a mean look, like he wanted to shoot ya just because he could."

"How long do you think it'll take us to get to you canyon tomorrow, John?" asked Calaveras.

"We leave here at first light; we should be there around midnight tomorrow. We'll have to swing south a ways. A couple of the canyons between here and there are too steep for the horses."

"Bigsby, you and Calaveras get some sleep. John and I'll split the first watch; we'll wake one of you in about four hours." Dumping his coffee on the ground, John cut a hunk of jerky from the piece in his saddlebag. Wrapping it in a piece of sacking, he put it back and picked up his rifle. He moved quietly into the shadows while Bigsby banked the fire.

"After all day in the saddle, this ground almost feels soft," said Calaveras as he stretched out on his blanket.

"Well then I must've got all the rocks," replied Bigsby.

John watched the two men for a few minutes before he moved off to the other side of the camp to keep watch.

****

"Rider coming in!" The cry from the lookout alerted the men below. Bowden, wakened early by the pain in his injured arm, knocked on the door to the shack. "Lookout reported a rider coming in," he said when Stewart opened the door. Shoving his feet into his boots, Stewart followed Bowden out towards the trail leading up from the road.

"It's Nelson," said Bowden. "Isn't he supposed to be in town with Sturgis?"

"Yes, he is. He'd better have a damn good reason for coming back this soon." Stewart was in a foul mood from being woken up this early.

Sliding his horse to stop in the rocky soil, Nelson jumped down from his horse. Dropping the reins, he quickly walked up to Stewart. "The Sheriff's planning a raid on the hide out. Sturgis said Doc Barton told him all about it."

"So where's Sturgis? Why isn't he here with you?" asked Stewart.

"Sturgis is dead. Mosebee shot him after we split up. He sent me to take care of the Doc and said he'd ride out to tell you what was going on. When I was coming back from the Doc's place I heard a shot behind the saloon. When I got there, I saw Mosebee standing over the body with a gun in his hand."

"What's this about Doc Barton?" asked Bowden.

"Sturgis said the reason Doc was talkin' so much was because he was drunk. He was afraid the old man would remember what he'd said when he sobered up, and tell the Sheriff. Told me to take care of him so I followed the Doc home. Found him passed out on his bed and smothered him so's not to make any noise. Towns folks'll figure the old coot died in his sleep."

"Alright, so what's this about the Sheriff planning to raid the hideout?" Stewart was wide awake now, and furious that a two-bit Sheriff with a tin star thought he could catch Jesse Stewart and his gang.

"All I know is what Sturgis said, that Sheriff Martin was getting a posse together and coming after you."

"So let him come. He'll be real sorry when finds we've out smarted him again." Striding towards the mine he started barking orders to his men.

"Willis, you, Jeeter, Hayes and Packard get the wagons hitched up and loaded with our gear. Get Cookie and get him to get his supplies together. I want you started towards the new place by noon. The rest of you men get your gear together and be ready to mount up in an hour."

"What new place, boss?" this was the first Nelson had heard of it.

"It's a place we figured on moving to when things got too hot around here," said Stewart. "You don't need to know where it is right now. After we finish with the town we'll head that way. That'll be soon enough for the rest of you to find out where it is."

"You're going after the town? Jesse, there ain't nothin' in that town worth stealin'. Hell, the bank probably don't have more'n a hunnert dollars in the safe." Nelson was obviously confused about Jesse's plans.

"Who said a damn thing about stealin' anything? I plan to burn the place down before we leave." Stewart had a wild look in his eye that Nelson hadn't seen before. "Sheriff thinks he can take us, so we'll just have to teach him a lesson. He's gonna have the only men in town brave or stupid enough to carry a gun with him, so there'll be no one left in town to stop us."

"Damn, Jesse, never thought of burnin' a whole town before. Just might be fun." Nelson began to smile as he headed over to the supply wagon to get a box of shells for his rifle.

With all the activity of getting the wagons loaded and the men ready to ride, no one paid any attention to Loomer as he slowly walked his horse down the trail to the road. He'd been hanging around the gang for about a month, coming and going at odd intervals, usually bringing in a deer or some rabbits or squirrels for Cookie to add to his stew. The men figured he was a little touched in the head so they pretty much left him alone. They had no idea he'd been spying on them, taking information back to Clay in Murieta.

Clay had told Loomer to find out what the gang was up to. As long as those plans didn't impact Murieta or his plans to purchase as much land in the area as he could, Clay didn't care what the gang did. Loomer was pretty sure that Stewart's plans to burn Murieta to the ground would get Clay's attention.

Once he reached the road, Loomer mounted his horse and started down the road, waving to the lookout as he passed. Once he was out of sight he turned off the road and took the old Indian trail he'd found back to town.

Chapter 16

Del Rogers and the Kid had been hanging around the town since yesterday afternoon and by now had a good idea something was up. Handsome had been seen driving a strange two-wheeled carriage out of town this morning. From the look of the cases he had strapped under the seat Del figured he was leaving town for a while. Fiddletown's Mercantile had done a brisk business earlier, but now had a closed sign hanging in the window.

There'd been a lot of commotion early this morning when Doc Barton had been found dead in his apartment. At first folks had said he'd died in his sleep, but now they were saying it looked like he'd been murdered.

The town was real quiet now, and Del knew it wasn't just because the Sheriff had told folks to go home. He'd seen several men over the last hour ride into town and go into the Sheriff's office; every single one of them wearing a six gun and carrying a rifle. Spotting the Kid over in front of the hotel, he waved him over.

"We need to find out what the Sheriff is up to," he said as the Kid stepped up to the boardwalk. "You stay here and keep an eye out. I'll get across the street down by the livery and sneak up on the jail from the alley. If I can get close enough to the window without being seen, I should be able to hear what they're planning."

"What should I do if they come out while you're sneakin' around?"

"Don't do nothin'. We'll let them ride out and then follow a ways to see where they're goin'. Once we know that, we'll split up and high tail it back to the hideout."

Del made sure no one was paying attention to him before he quickly crossed the street to the livery. Ducking down below the backs of the horses, he trotted to the back of the corral. Turning into the alley he pulled his pistol; and, walking carefully, moved to the back of the jail. A small window opened onto the narrow gap between buildings, and he could hear the voices of the men inside. He crept closer to the window, but before he could make out what they were saying, he felt the cold muzzle of a Colt hit him in the back of the neck.

"Drop the gun, Del, real easy like. That's fine. Now get your hands up, nice and slow." Del complied with the orders from Deputy Johnson then heard him take a step back. "Alright now walk straight ahead."

As they moved up the walkway to the street, Del asked "How'd you know I was there?"

"Sheriff saw you and the other fella hangin' round, figured you was spyin' for Stewart. Had me and a couple others staked out, waitin' to see when you'd show up. Now, you wanted to see the Sheriff so let's go!" Turning left at the street, Deputy Johnson walked his prisoner to the door of the jail. "Open up, Sheriff, its Ben. I got Rogers."

When the door opened, Ben shoved Del through. Before it closed Del looked towards the hotel but saw no sign of the Kid. Catching his look, Sheriff Martin chuckled. "Don't worry about your partner, Del. We'll take care of him too. Now drop that belt. We got a cell in back with your name on it. When the circuit judge gets here, we'll have a nice fair trail for you."

"On what charge? You got nothin' on me, Sheriff."

"Bill, is this him?" Looking at a stout man standing by the wall, Martin nodded at his prisoner.

"Yes sir, that's him. Him and three others was the ones attacked us two months back, beat me half to death and stole our horses and cattle. Said if we called in the law they'd come back and kill us all." Bill still had a bad limp and scars on his face from the brutal beating he'd received.

"I'd say the charges are attempted murder, horse theft and extortion. Looks like you're going to hang, Del." Taking the keys off the wall peg, Martin walked Del into the cell and locked him in.

Watching from across the street, the Kid saw Deputy Johnson take Del captive and deliver him to the jail. It was time for him to get out of town and warn

Stewart. Looked like folks in this town were startin' to grow courage and that meant the days of easy pickin's was over. Straightening up, he turned away from the street and went around the corner to where his horse was tied at the rail. He stepped into the stirrup and was just starting to swing his leg over when he heard someone behind him.

"Stop right there Kid, get back off that horse, nice and slow."

Instead of stopping, the Kid threw himself over the top of his horse, grabbed his rifle and hit the ground in a roll. Jumping to his feet, he fired a shot at the man on the other side as his horse shied, and then he turned and ran for the corner. A slug from a pistol tore splinters from the wall inches from his head as he disappeared.

"Dammit," shouted Tim Giles as he grabbed the side of his head. The bullet from the Kid's rifle had come within a whisker of killing him; slicing off the top of his ear instead. Pulling off his bandana, he quickly tied it around his head then took off after the outlaw. Stopping to look around the corner, he saw Sheriff Martin and Deputy Johnson coming out of the jail.

"Tim, are you all right?"

"Yeah, the son of a bitch just nicked me. I think he went behind the store. He managed to get his rifle off his horse, Sheriff, so be careful."

"Alright, I'll take the far side 'n see if I can flush him back to you." Keeping low, Martin ran across the street towards the front of the bank. Tim heard the heavy report of a rifle and saw the shot throw dirt in the air near the Sheriff. Smoke showed him the Kid was hunkered down behind some crates lining the boardwalk in front of the store. It was going to be almost impossible to get him from the street without getting shot.

Moving fast, Tim ran to the back of the hotel and then crossed the street to the back of the mercantile. Finding the back door unlocked, he went inside where he found himself in a storeroom. Ahead was a heavy curtain separating the storeroom from the main part of the store. Carefully pulling the edge of the curtain back, he could see through the store to the front windows. The Kid could just be seen hiding behind the crates to the right of the door.

Tim moved slowly through the store, stepping softly to keep his boot heels from hitting the board floor and alerting the Kid. When he reached the front door of the store, he looked again. The Kid was still in the same spot. Taking a deep breath Tim yanked open the door and yelled "Hands up, Kid!"

As he'd expected, the Kid jumped to his feet and turned, bringing the rifle around to shoot. Before Tim could pull the trigger on his pistol a rifle shot rang out from across the street. The Kid spun against the wall of the store, dropping the rifle and grabbing at his side. Blood rapidly turned his shirt red where the heavy slug from the Deputy's rifle had caught him. Kicking the rifle out of reach, Tim pulled the pistol from the Kid's belt and tossed it back into the store.

"I been shot! The damn Deputy actually shot me!" The Kid gave Tim a surprised look and then slumped unconscious against the front of the store. Pulling the Kid's bandana loose, Tim held it against the wound and called out, "Its clear Sheriff. The Kid's down."

"Is he dead?" asked the Sheriff as he ran up.

"No, just passed out. It's bad, Sheriff; and with the Doc killed, I don't think he'll last long."

"Well, let's get him over to the livery and have Sally see what she can do to stop the bleeding. We can shackle him to the bed in case he comes to. Ben, send a telegram to lone. See if they can send a doctor."

Standing up, Sheriff Martin put a hand on his Deputy's shoulder. "Look, Ben, I know you want to come with us on this; but I need someone I can trust to stay here in town in case there are any more of Stewart's men in town."

"I understand Sheriff. Besides, with this rib, I wouldn't be able ride very far anyway. I'll make sure these two stay locked up till you get back."

"Thanks, Ben. If this plan works, by tomorrow night we'll be able to put an end to Stewart and his attacks on innocent people." Picking up his Winchester, Martin walked to his horse and headed out to meet up with the rest of the posse waiting on the outskirts of town.

"Walter, is everybody here?" he asked as he rode up to the group of men waiting by the Henson's water tanks.

"We're all here, Sheriff. "

"Good. Walter, Frank, we're going to take the road up as far as the trail to Scotts Creek. We'll cut across there and hit the road that runs by the old mines at Indian Diggin's. There we wait for Handsome's signal."

****

Stewart sat on his horse and watched the last of the wagons roll down road towards the new hideout. Nelson was nearby; rolling himself a cigarette as he sat his horse. Snapping a match alight with a gnarled thumbnail he lit his smoke then flipped the match away.

"When you plannin' to hit the town, Jesse?"

"Tomorrow afternoon. Del and the Kid haven't come back yet, so I figure the Sheriff must've recognized them and they're either dead or in jail. That probably means the Sheriff will try to hit us tomorrow morning."

"How you figure that?"

"We know he's gettin' a posse together; and, since he's most likely taken out Del and the Kid, he figures he's got time to get ready. He's not gonna want to try and hit us in broad daylight, so I figure he'll try to sneak up on us at first light. We'll leave Dusty here as a lookout. That way they won't realize we're gone, and he might actually shoot some of them if they get close."

"And he'll most likely get himself killed as well," remarked Nelson. "How do we not run into the Sheriff and his posse on our way to the town?"

"Dusty gets himself killed, that's his problem. We'll head east on the road about half a mile then turn south and cross Jackson Road before turning back north. We can cross the river and come into town from the west. I've got some of the men making torches now. We light them after we cross the river and make a run down the street firing as many buildings as we can. They'll be too busy fightin' the fires to come after us, and by the time the Sheriff gets back with his posse we'll be long gone."

Chapter 17

It was just after midnight when Bigsby and his three friends walked their horses up the narrow canyon south of where Indian Creek joined up with Scott Creek. As they came to the edge of the small clearing they stopped and waited, listening carefully. After few minutes of hearing nothing but the night critters going about their business, they entered the small pocket of grass screened by pines and manzanita.

"There's water from a seep over by the rocks, so we can picket the horses here," said John quietly.

"How far is it from here?" asked Bigsby.

"About a quarter mile into the canyon, then about a hundred yards almost straight up. I figure it'll take us a couple of hours to get to the top of the ridge. That'll give us about an hour to find the lookout. Handsome should start his distraction about then, and we can take care of the lookout quietly."

After taking care of the horses, they followed John to the north end of the clearing. There behind some boulders they saw the entrance to the slot canyon.

"You sure we can make it through there?" asked Calaveras. "All I see is a crack in the rock!"

"It's a real tight squeeze for about ten feet, then it opens up," said John. "Once past that it's about four or five feet wide the rest of the way."

"Wonderful," said Bigsby. Picking up his rifle and canteen, he said "Lead on. We can't accomplish anything just standing around here."

Two hours later the sky was showing the first hint of color in the east as the three men pulled themselves over the edge of the canyon. Dirt caked their faces, and their arms were quivering from the exertion of the climb.

"Damn, John," whispered Calaveras hoarsely, "you weren't kidding when you said it was about straight up!"

"That weren't nothin' but a little exercise Ladies," said John, a slight smile on his face. He'd set a hard pace up the canyon wall and was impressed that they'd all made it without faltering.

"We've got about an hour to find the lookout and take him out," said Bigsby as he checked his pistols and rifle. "Handsome is set to make his play at sun up, so we need to be ready."

"According to what we found out, the lookout should be on the point about a quarter mile north east of here," said John. "There's a steep gully to cross that's full of dry brush and manzanita. We need to be careful we don't make any noise crossing it."

"Is there anyway around it we can make before dawn?" asked Calaveras. "Bigsby and I are gonna have a rough time getting through thick brush quietly."

"I think if we drop down into the gully here, then go uphill about two hundred yards, there's a spot where the brush thins out almost all the way to the ridge line," said John. "We often use it to get around a deer or bear we're tracking."

"OK, we need to get moving," said Bigsby. "John, you lead, I'll cover us."

****

Handsome had decided several hours ago that this was with out a doubt the most embarrassing thing he had ever let Bigsby talk him into. Out here alone, not a quarter mile from the hideout of one of the most notorious outlaws in the county, he was about to make a most ungentlemanly spectacle of himself.

"Bigsby," he swore under his breath, "you and I are definitely going to have to re-evaluate our friendship after this. I do believe you have come to rely much too much upon my generosity of spirit."

Opening the trunk attached to the back of the carriage, Handsome began removing the petticoats, gown, and wig Sally had loaned him for this part of the plan. He'd removed the burlap wrapped around the horse's hooves to muffle the sound of their iron shoes, but he'd left the rags woven through the harnesses to keep them from jingling as the horses moved.

"Bear in mind, Handsome, if these clothes get damaged in any way you'll be responsible for replacing them!" Sally had told him with a barely suppressed grin.

"Ma'am, I do feel you're questioning my honor by saying such a thing. I'm a gentleman of my word, and I assure you that these fine garments will be returned to you in pristine condition." Handsome was finding it harder and harder to hang onto what dignity he could in front of Sally, and wanted nothing more than to make as dignified an exit as was possible under the present conditions.

Sitting in the carriage, trying to get the blasted wig on straight and keeping his gun from getting tangled in the gown, Handsome waited impatiently for the dawn.

****

Dusty, who'd had the moniker hung on him for his tendency to get thrown off his horse, was bored and cold. He hated guard duty, especially when there was nothing to guard.

"Don't know why they need a damn lookout when everybody's done gone 'n left the place," he groused. But Stewart had told him to stay, and he feared Stewart enough to stay put. Lighting another smoke, he waited miserably, continuing to quietly curse his lousy luck.

Less than a hundred yards away, John held up his hand in warning. "You smell that, Bigsby?" he whispered.

"Wood smoke? I don't understand. Why would a lookout give away his position like that?"

"He wouldn't. I don't like this at all." Bigsby could see that John was worried.

"You thinking ambush, John?" asked Calaveras.

"Nah, if they were trying to trap us, they wouldn't do something guaranteed to make us suspicious," said Bigsby. John nodded in agreement.

"Let me try something," said Tom as he quietly handed his rifle to Calaveras. "Hold onto this. I shouldn't need more'n about fifteen minutes." Pulling his pistol, Tom silently disappeared into the dark.

As the sun finally started to spread its crimson light over the tops of the hills, Dusty stubbed out his smoke and hauled himself to his feet. Limping over to the edge of the canyon to relieve himself, he let his gaze wander over the valley below.

He was buttoning his trousers when his eyes spotted movement on the road below. "Now what on earth is that?" he asked himself. Hurrying back to his bedroll, he picked up a small telescope.

Focusing on the movement he'd seen earlier, he was startled by what he saw. "Now just what in the hell is she doing out here?" he wondered. Putting down the telescope he thought hard. Stewart had made it very clear that no one was to approach the mine without first giving the signal. If anyone dared, they were to be shot, no questions asked. He wasn't happy about having to shoot no woman, but that wasn't anything compared to what he'd been threatened with if he didn't follow orders.

Raising his rifle to shoot, he heard a twig snap behind him. Spinning to his left, he hardly had time to recognize the shape coming at him before Tom's fist crashed into his jaw. Dusty crumpled, unconscious, to the ground.

"My compliments to your friend, Bigsby," said Tom. "His distraction was just what we needed."

"That may be true," said Bigsby, smiling at Calaveras. "However, I have a feeling Handsome would rather not talk about it." As John and Tom tied up the helpless lookout, Calaveras doused the small fire.

"Better send Handsome the signal," he told Bigsby.

"Just about to do that," replied Bigsby as he pulled a square of red cloth from his pocket. Attaching it to a branch he walked to the edge of the cliff and started waving it over his head, keeping a large tree between himself and Stewart's hideout.

"It's about damn time, Bigsby," muttered Handsome as he saw the signal on the ridge. Stripping off the wig and shawl, he stood up in the carriage and stepped out of the bustled dress he'd borrowed from Sally at the livery. He still flushed red remembering the laughter as he'd explained his part in the plan. Tossing the clothes in the bottom of the carriage, he grabbed the reins and the short whip. "Haw," he whispered, urging the horses into a canter. He had to get to the Sheriff waiting up the canyon about a mile away as soon as he could. With the noise of the horse and carriage wheels on the rocky ground, he sincerely hoped that Stewart's men were not prone to be early risers.

"We need to get down to the road and meet the Sheriff, Bigsby," said John. "There's something not right about this, and we need to find out what it is before that posse goes riding up to the hideout."

"I agree," said Bigsby. "Calaveras, tie this guy to that tree and gag him. We'll come back and get him after we see what's going on down there."

While Calaveras grabbed a length of rope from Dusty's gear, Bigsby, Tom and John scrambled as quietly down the ridge to the road as they could. Calaveras joined them a couple of minutes later just as they heard horses being walked slowly up the road.

"Sheriff, it's me, Bigsby." His words were soft but carried clearly. Moving quickly, the Sheriff stepped off his horse and joined him under the branches of a straggly pine hanging partially over the road.

"What is it, trouble?" asked Sheriff Martin.

"Don't know. The lookout had a fire going. Didn't seem too worried it might give him away." Bigsby filled the Sheriff in on what they suspected as the rest of the posse and his three friends joined them.

"It might be a trap, but it doesn't feel that way," concluded Bigsby. "Sheriff, I think you, Calaveras, John, Tom, Handsome and myself should take a look up ahead before we decide what to do. Just a few of us will be quieter."

"You're right, Bigsby." Turning, Sheriff Martin picked out Bill Turner standing nearby. "Bill, keep the men here, but out of sight under the trees. We'll signal when we want you to join us. Of course, if you hear shooting, I expect you come a running with guns blazing!"

"I concur," added Handsome. However I would appreciate it if you only shoot the outlaws."

"Sure thing, Sheriff," said Bill, giving Handsome a funny look. While he was gathering the posse, the six men began to cautiously move towards the hideout.

When they'd gone about two hundred yards, John motioned for them to stop. "Sheriff, this small stream flows out of a spring next to the mine. If we stay next to the bushes, we can come up behind the mine shack out of sight of the mine entrance."

Bigsby nodded in agreement and the men continued towards the camp. Stopping again about twenty yards away from the mine shack, they watched from a clump of manzanita. There was no sign of movement or smoke from the shacks chimney. In fact the place had a deserted feel to it.

"Sheriff, you, Tom and I'll go around to the left and check out the shack," said Bigsby softly. "Calaveras, you take John and Handsome and check out the mine. It looks like the place has been abandoned, but let's not take any chances. Give a whistle when you're in position, and we'll hit both at once."

"Good idea. Give us about five minutes to get over there." Calaveras pulled his pistol to check the loads and then moved off with Handsome and John close behind him.

Chapter 18

Bigsby, along with Tom and Sheriff Martin, quietly made their way to the front of the cabin. From there they could see the crude fence the outlaws had thrown together to make a corral for their horses. It stood empty, the makeshift gate lying on the ground. They saw a couple of empty whiskey bottles on the ground near the door of the cabin, but nothing to indicate anyone was still living there.

As Calaveras, Handsome and Tom approached the mine entrance, they too saw no signs to indicate it was occupied. There was no morning fire, nor any of the usual equipment you saw at an encampment. Giving a low whistle, they stood up; and, with guns in hand, moved quickly to the mine.

Hearing the whistle, Sheriff Martin kicked open the door and rushed into the shack, closely followed by the other two.

"They've cleared out," he shouted towards the others at the mine.

"Same here, Sheriff," answered Tom.

Joining the others at the mine, it was apparent
to Bigsby that Stewart's gang wasn't planning to return
anytime soon.
"Stewart must've found out we were coming,"
said Handsome.

"Unless he has a spy we don't know about, I
don't see how," said Sheriff Martin. "We were careful
and none of these men talked it about."

Murmurs of agreement came from the men,
and then Walter Brack asked, "Where do you suppose
they've gone Sheriff?"

"I have no idea," he answered.

"But we may have someone who does!" Bigsby
looked for Tom and waved him over. "Tom, take
Handsome with you and bring back the lookout we left
tied up. I'll bet he has an idea where they might be."

As Tom and Handsome headed back down the
trail to the road, Sheriff Martin turned back to Brack.

"Walter, I got a bad feeling about this. Until we
can talk to that fellow they captured, take some of the
men and check around the area. See if you can find
tracks of a large group headed away from here. The
rest of you grab some torches and check out the mine.
See if they might have left anything back there that
can help us. John and I'll go over the shack again.

Twenty minutes later after a fruitless search,
Martin and John were standing out front of the shack

when they heard Handsome and Tom returning with their captive. Shouting for the men in the mine to join them, he watched the three men approach. As they got closer, he recognized Dusty.

"I know you," he said. "Handsome, this here's Dusty. He rides with Stewart's gang. Take that gag outta his mouth and let's see what he has to say."

Dusty still looked pretty wobbly, and it was apparent from his condition that he hadn't actually "walked" down the hill from where they'd had him tied up. Even so, he wasn't inclined to be very helpful.

"Ya got no proof I was ever with that gang, Sheriff. I was just camped for the night before movin' on." He said.

"I recognize him too, Sheriff," called Frank Pratt. "He was one of the men jumped my partner 'n me over by Dry Creek. I recognize that hat of his!"

"That so?" asked the Sheriff.

"He's lyin'," exclaimed Dusty. "I stole this hat off some saddle tramp over by Sutter's Mill."

"Who you callin' a liar, you low down varmint?" Several men grabbed Frank before he could do more than land a solid punch to the side of Dusty's head.

"Hold on there, Frank," said Martin. "Let us handle this. We'll find out the truth."

"We sure will, Sheriff," said Bigsby. Catching Calaveras's eye he got an answering nod. "Let's let Calaveras see if he can get this polecat to talk."

"Are you quite certain you want this, Bigsby?" asked Handsome, looking nervously at Calaveras. "You do recall what happened to that fellow down near Sonora, don't you?"

"What're you worried about, Handsome? That horse thief deserved what he got." While Bigsby was talking, Calaveras walked over to where Dusty could see him. Pretending not to look at the outlaw, he proceeded to pull a huge knife from the sheath on his belt. Inspecting it carefully, he began to hone the edge on his leather cuff.

"Correct, the miscreant did deserve to be punished; but he should have been hung. To die that way is inhuman, no matter the crime that has been perpetrated." It was clear Handsome was bothered by what had happened to the criminal.

"What's he talkin' about?" asked Dusty, not taking his eyes off the knife Calaveras was still playing with.

"Seems this fellow refused to be co-operative when asked about his partner's whereabouts," said Handsome. "When the local constabulary got tired of his refusal to talk, Calaveras offered to get the information for them. My understanding is that the poor unfortunate was skinned almost to the waist before he decided to talk. I hear it took him an unusually long time to succumb to his injuries."

"What'd he just say?" asked Dusty, clearly confused by the long words being used.

"He said Calaveras used that knife on the guy till he talked, and that it took him a long time to die," answered Bigsby.

"Hold him up for me, Bigsby," said Calaveras as he moved towards Dusty and grabbed the front of his shirt. Looking into the outlaws eyes, he brought the knife up and gently pressed the tip into the underside of his jaw. "Now we don't have a lot of time, so I suggest you save yourself some pain and just tell us what we'd like to know."

"I can't!." wailed Dusty. "You got any idea what Stewart'll do to me if I talk?"

"No, but I know what I'm going to do if you don't," answered Calaveras.   Turning the point of the knife down, he easily split the vest and rough cloth shirt from Dusty's collar to his waist.

"Now hold on here….." Sheriff Martin started to object. Bigsby laid a hand on his arm and shook his head. The Sheriff stopped, but Bigsby could see he wasn't happy.

"I still ain't sayin' nuthin'," blustered Dusty, though you could see from his eyes he was pretty near scared to death.

"Sorry to hear that, Dusty," sighed Calaveras as he placed the tip of the knife in the hollow of Dusty's throat, applying just the tiniest bit of pressure.

Dusty screamed and jerked his head back as he felt the knife pierce the skin on his neck. "Alright, alright, I'll talk," he wailed. Sobbing, he hung in the arms of his captors as he pleaded with them. "Make him stop. I'll tell you everything I know."

"You tell us first Dusty; and then we'll decide," said Bigsby. He nodded to Calaveras who stepped back but kept the knife where Dusty could see it.

"When Bowden told Stewart what'd happened at the Eldritch place, he must of figured you was up to somethin', Sheriff. He sent a couple of guys into town to see if they could learn anything. While they was gone, Nelson came back all excited about something. Didn't hear what. Stewart, he started yellin' and had Jeeter and three others start packing everything up." Dusty was talking so fast he was difficult to understand. "When they was done, he sent them off with the gear; but I don't know where they went. He never told us."

"Slow down a little, Dusty. Let me get this straight. Only some of you knew where Stewart was going?" Sheriff Martin seemed puzzled by this.

"That's right, Sheriff. Said we'd be told when we needed to know. After they was gone, when Del and the Kid never showed, he seemed real mad. Told folks to get their gear and be ready to move out. Told me to go up on the ridge and keep a lookout. Next thing I know, I saw the whole damn bunch of 'em riding outta here."

"Which way did they go?" asked Tom.

"They went east," answered Dusty. He sounded a little less scared, but he still kept both eyes on Calaveras. "But I think they didn't stay on the road."

"Why's that?" asked the Sheriff.

"When folks is on the road headed east, you can hear 'em for at least a mile. Something to do with the shape of the canyon I was told. Anyways, they hadn't had time to git that far before I couldn't hear 'em no more."

"That means they headed cross country, Sheriff," said John. "Only reason I can see them doing that is they must've known we were coming."

Looking stunned, Sheriff Martin sprang to his feet. "Walter, get everybody together. I think Stewart's planning to hit the town!"

"Are you sure about that, Sheriff?" Walter hesitated, clearly confused by the Sheriff's orders.

"Think about it, Walter," shouted Martin as he ran for his horse. "If he knew we were coming after him, then he'd know there wouldn't be anyone in town that'd stand up to him."

"Damn him! You're right! Come on men!" Walter jumped on his horse and started rounding the others up.

As they headed out, Sheriff Martin stopped where Bigsby and the others stood with Dusty. "Come as quick as you can, men. We're going to need all the help we can get." Spurring his horse, he headed down the road without waiting for a reply.

"Handsome, you still have the carriage. Take Dusty and get back to town as soon as you can. It'll probably take us a couple of hours to get back to where we left our horses. I doubt we'll be back in town before dark."

"Alright, Bigsby. Since you seem to have planned this all along, I'll foray into danger while you and your friends take a leisurely stroll through the woods." Handsome tossed a jaunty wave to his friends before grabbing the rope around Dusty's wrists. "Come with me you despicable cretin. Perhaps during our perilous ride into town you can learn a thing or two about manners and bravery."

"Does your friend always talk like that?" asked Tom as they started back towards the slot canyon and their mounts.

"Usually, yes," answered Calaveras. "But sometimes he can get carried away."

"Not sure I'd want to be near when that happens," muttered Tom. "Man could get a real mean headache if'n he had to listen to that for very long." As the other men laughed, Tom looked at Calaveras. "You wouldn't really have skinned that hombre, would you?"

"Naw," chuckled Calaveras. I limit my skinning to animals, not men."

"So I take it the story about the fellow in Sonora....?"

"Just a well timed story on Handsomes' part. All I did was play along. I figure Dusty's own imagination did the rest."

Having broken the tension they all felt at not being able to ride with the Sheriff and his posse, the four men pressed on, eager to reach the bottom of the canyon where their horses waited.

Chapter 19

Clay was walking across the street towards the hotel when he looked up and saw Loomer riding towards him on a heavily lathered horse. Reining the exhausted animal to a stop, he started to tell Clay his news.

"Not here in the middle of the street, you fool," said Clay.

"It's real important, Clay," stammered Loomer in his excitement. "Stewart and his gang are planning to attack the town!"

Stunned, Clay wheeled on Loomer, causing the man to take a step back.

"Are you sure about this? When is he coming?" Up till now he'd figured that Stewart was content to harass the ranchers and miners in the surrounding territory and leave the town alone. He was a lot less likely to get the townsfolk riled up enough to form a posse that way. Plus, he was making it easier for Clay to get those same ranchers to sell out cheap rather than face the possibility of further attacks. Directly attacking the town like this was the last thing he'd expected Stewart to try.

"I ain't sure, Mr. Francis; but I figure sometime today. He's moving his hideout, but I couldn't hear where to. He plans to burn the place down if'n he can!"

"Damn, he must've found out about the Sheriff's plan to hit his hideout this morning! I can't think of any other reason he'd do something like this." Clay was thinking fast. If Stewart succeeded, his plans would be useless; the property he'd already purchased would be worthless.

"Loomer, your horse is done. Take mine and get out to my place and have Taggert round up his men and meet me at the livery in two hours."

"Yes Sir, Mr. Francis." Loomer wheeled his horse around to the rail and jumped from the saddle. Wrapping the reins around the rail with one hand, he pulled the reins loose on Clay's horse, swung into the saddle and headed towards the old Wilson place.

As Loomer headed out of town, Clay changed course and made for the Sheriff's office. He didn't know if Deputy Johnson had made the connection between Red and himself or not; but either way, he had to let the Deputy know what was coming. The money loss would hurt, but with innocent women and children in danger, his sense of honor would not allow him to walk away and leave the town to its fate.

Opening the door to the jail, Clay startled the Deputy who was eating breakfast at the desk. Jumping out of the chair to avoid the spilled coffee, Ben grabbed for his handkerchief and started mopping up the mess.

"Dag-nabbit! Look what ya done made me do!" Ben had been looking at some papers on the desk, and now was trying pick them out of the coffee before they got wet. "Sheriff Martin's gonna be mad at me for this, and it weren't my fault!"

"Deputy, I recommend you forget about the papers and listen." Clay's voice was stern and commanding, making Ben stop and look at him.

"What is it, Mr. Francis? What's wrong?" Ben had a sinking feeling in his stomach as he looked at Clay. He knew the Sheriff was concerned about the rumors he'd heard about the man, but as Sheriff Martin had told him, without proof there wasn't anything they could do.

"I've just gotten word that Stewart and his gang are planning to attack the town today. I believe they plan to burn it to the ground if they can. We need to get every man that can hold a gun to meet at the livery, and we need to get the women and children somewhere where they'll be safe."

"Burn the town? You ain't serious are ya? Stewarts never bothered the town directly before."

"That's because Sheriff Martin has never tried to attack Stewart directly before, you idiot. He found out what was going on and planned to attack while the Sheriff and his posse are too far away to do anything about it. Now get that chain off the rifle rack then get out there and start rounding folks up. I'd recommend you have the women and children watch for any fires that might get started."

Clay waited until Ben had unlocked the chain on the rifle rack and then pushed the Deputy towards the door. As he began to gather the half dozen Winchesters, he turned to the Deputy who was still standing in the doorway.

"What are you waiting for man? We don't know exactly when Stewart is going to get here, so we have no time to waste. Send a couple of men back here for the shotguns and shells, and send someone over to the mercantile to get as many rifles and as much ammunition as they can find. Have them bring it all over to the livery, where we can figure out the best way to defend the town."

"How do you know all this, Mr. Francis? How do you know what Stewart is planning?" Ben was still suspicious and wasn't ready to blindly follow along.

"Because I had someone watching them, that's how. If there was going to be a problem with the gang, I wanted to know about it before it happened. As long as they left the town and my holdings alone, I had no issue with them. But now they're a threat to both. So either help me get ready to defend the town or get the hell out of the way!" Pushing past the still hesitant Deputy, Clay left the jail and headed towards the livery.

Watching Clay walk down the boardwalk, Ben made a decision. He had to put the safety of the people and the town first. That was the oath he'd taken when the Sheriff had pinned the Deputy's badge on him. After they'd finished with the business today, then he'd deal with whatever else it might be that Mr. Francis was doing.

"Alright, I'll send a telegram to Sheriff Williams in Ione, Mr. Francis. I'll also put a couple of men about a mile outside of town to watch for Stewart and give us a little warning."

"Good. Since Stewart is threatening to burn the town, I'd get some men to fill as many water buckets and barrels as we can find. Set them up around town where they'll be handy if any fires do get started."

Chapter 20

Tired and covered with mud and scratches from their headlong rush back to their horses, the four men emerged from the mouth of the slot canyon about mid-morning, scattering birds and rabbits from the clearing. Stopping only long enough to get a drink of water and wipe some of the dirt from their faces, the four men untied their horses and mounted up.

"If we head southwest over the ridge, we'll pick up an old Indian trail on the other side," said John. "We follow that back and it'll save us at least a couple of hours."

"That'll get us to town before dark," replied Bigsby. "Sheriff Martin's going to need help if Stewart is after the town. I figure we cross the river then come in from behind the livery until we know what's going on. Don't want to get shot by some excited storekeeper thinking we're the bad guys."

Glancing over his shoulder to make sure they were ready, John tapped his horse's ribs with his spurs and started through the trees towards the ridge.

Half an hour later they crossed the ridge and started down towards the trail. Walking the horses now to give them a rest, Bigsby and Calaveras were talking quietly as they followed John and Tom down the slope.

"We should've known Stewart had spies in town, Calaveras. We left those folks defenseless while we're out here where we can't help!"

"Don't beat yourself up, Bigsby. We knew it was pretty likely that there were some of Stewart's lackeys in town, but I think we did a pretty good of keeping our plans quiet. Besides, Ben Johnson's in town, and there're several other good men there as well."

"I know, and you're right, Ben is a good man. But he's injured, and they have no idea anyone's coming. Hell, Stewart and his men could gun down half the folks in the street before they knew what hit them."

"Look, Bigsby, Sheriff Martin and his posse should be getting to town in about two hours, and with this short cut we shouldn't be more'n a couple hours behind them."

"Let's see if we can make it less," said Bigsby. Urging his horse he rode forward.

John looked at Bigsby as he rode up beside him, and then nodded. Without speaking, the men moved off through the trees at a trot.

****

Clay had his men spread out across the rooftops of the buildings where the Jackson Road came into town. It was the most likely route for Stewart to take, provided he was as hot-headed as folks claimed. If he was, he'd be too interested in seeing how much damage he could do to try something other than a frontal attack. But just to cover his bets, Clay had a couple men on horseback outside of town as lookouts.

He'd gotten the store owners to provide the ammunition for the men defending the town, as well as buckets and tubs for water. The rough board planks of the buildings were mostly unpainted and tinder dry, and if they were to have any chance to save the town from fire they weren't going to have time to find water buckets after the fire started. Now every building had water handy, and the women and older children had been charged with watching for fire.

With the help of Art, Bryce and Ben Johnson they had everyone pretty well organized and as ready as they could get them. Clay's men would try to take the brunt of the attack, while those unfamiliar with firearms were in the shops along the street, most with shotguns. Their job would be to keep the outlaws that got into town from making it inside the buildings and setting fires.

Standing at the end of the street with Deputy Johnson, Clay looked around the town. Except for the rifle barrels sticking out from behind the building facades and the upper floor of the hotel and saloon, the town looked deserted. No horses were at any of the rails, and even the stray dogs that were always about scavenging for scraps were missing.

"I'd imagine that if Stewart gets close enough to see there's no one about he'd know something was up. Shouldn't we at least have some of the men moving about so he don't get suspicious?" Ben was nervously wiping his hands on his vest as he talked, unable to keep them still.

"Actually, were better off if he does get suspicious, Ben. I'd prefer he think twice about trying to burn the town and just ride off," answered Clay, lighting a cigar with a wooden match he'd pulled from a vest pocket.

"You really think he'd do that, Clay?" asked Ben.

"From what I've heard of this outlaw, probably not. However, if there is a chance to avoid this conflict, I see no reason not to try it. If Stewart attacks, men are going to die today. If we're lucky, it'll be his men and not ours; and the town will be saved. And perhaps if we're even luckier, Sheriff Martin will arrive before Stewart's gang."

"I don't think that'll happen, Clay. They weren't supposed to even be at the hideout until just after dawn."

"Then I guess we'll just have to handle this ourselves, won't we Deputy?" Turning away from Ben, Clay walked towards the livery where Art and Bryce were watching the road from behind a couple of freight wagons pulled up in front.

Chapter 21

Tommy Jacobs was scared. Not so much of the outlaws, cause after all, he was sure they wouldn't hurt a little kid. He was really worried about what his Ma was going to say when she found out he wasn't home with his little sister. When he'd overheard the men talk about the Stewart gang, he'd asked Mr. Standeford to let him ride out with them.

"Not this time, Tommy. This is something very dangerous, and you need to let the men handle it. Now go on home and help your Ma look after your sister." Tommy had been disappointed but determined to help. He'd decided then that he wasn't going to go home and hide with the girls!

Sitting on the big draft horse under the branches of a live oak, Tommy watched the road a hundred yards away near the bottom of the valley. He was about a quarter of a mile further out than one of the men Mr. Francis had sent out, so if the Stewart gang came this way he was going to see them first. He knew his horse wasn't fast, but all he had to do was get to the lookout around the bend at the west end of the valley.

After several minutes, Tommy got tired of sitting on the big horse and jumped down. Walking over to the trunk of the tree, he found a spot where he could get comfortable and still see the road. The air was heavy and warm, filled with the songs of the birds and low hum of insects gathering nectar from the flowering bushes nearby. The scents of the flowers and the trees filled his nose as he concentrated on watching the road.

Until the sound of a horse's shoe hitting a rock jerked him awake, Tommy had no idea he'd fallen asleep. Panicked, he looked around, starting to get to his feet until a movement to his right froze him in place. Not thirty yards away, a mounted man was walking his horse quietly through the trees. Another followed not far behind, and from the sounds there were more he couldn't see. Unable to move, little Tommy watched as several men came out of the trees and gathered along the road. He was sure they were the outlaws, even though he'd never seen any of them in town before.

Finally able to overcome his fright enough to get his arms and legs moving again, Tommy crept up to his horse, praying as hard as he could the darn nag would be quiet and not give him away. Grabbing the reins and a handful of the horses mane, he jumped as hard as he could and got his chest and stomach onto the horses back. Holding his breath when the horse tossed it's head and turned to look at him, he squirmed quickly to get his leg over the broad back and then pushed himself upright.

Looking down into the valley, he saw some of the men had gotten off their horses and were huddled in a group. He saw that several of them were holding sticks but had no idea what they were doing until he saw one man light a match and hold it to the end of a stick. When it burst into flames, Tommy gasped. Torches! They were lighting torches! And since it was the middle of the day, that could only mean they were going to burn the town!

Pulling the reins hard, he turned his horse towards the end of the valley and hammered his bare heels into its ribs as hard as he could. Surprised by his actions, the horse whinnied loudly and broke into a gallop, crashing through the brush and trees. Hanging on to the horses mane with all his might, eyes closed tight, Tommy didn't see the startled looks of the men on the road or the rifles three of them pointed in his direction. Tommy didn't hear the reports as the men shot at his running shadow, but did hear the snapping whine of several bullets by his head. Daring a glimpse behind him as his horse topped a small knoll, he saw that all the men were mounted and coming his way. Oh boy, his Ma was really gonna be mad at him now!

Willy Burke heard the shots and men yelling and was turning his horse to ride hard for the town when he saw a horse come galloping over the knoll hiding the bend in the road. At first he couldn't make out the strange shape on its back, but then it resolved itself into the shape of a small boy. Looking closer, he recognized the Jacobs draft horse and then Tommy, hanging on as tight as he could.

"What on earth is that damn kid doing out here riding that plug bareback?" he muttered to himself. "There's no way in hell that nag can outrun those men." Without hesitating he spurred his horse towards the oncoming pair.

"Tommy," he yelled. When the boy looked up, he waved. "Over here! Its me, Will Burke." Guiding his horse next to Tommy's, Will reached out and plucked the boy off the horse and swung him over to his. Settling the young boy behind him, Will shouted for him to hang on and whipped his horse into a run away from the oncoming men. Splashing across the creek, they charged up the hill towards the town.

"You okay, Tommy?" Will asked as they reached to top of the hill. The town could be seen below them, maybe a half mile away. Will quickly pulled his rifle from its scabbard and fired three quick shots into the air, the signal they'd agreed on earlier.

"I'm okay, Mr. Burke. Are those men the outlaws you were looking for?"

"Yes they are, Tommy. What were you doing out here?"

"I was trying to help. I'm not a little kid, but nobody thought I could do anything to help. When I saw the men chasing us, they were lighting torches. Are they really going to burn down the town?"

"They're going to try, Tommy, but I think we're ready for them. You just be ready to jump off when I get to the livery, and then you get your behind home." Will couldn't blame the kid for wanting to help, but he'd sure picked a lousy time for it.

"Yessir, Mr. Burke. I'll do that for sure," said Tommy.

Looking back over his shoulder, Will saw they had about a four hundred yard lead on the gang. It was going to be pretty close.

Chapter 22

Sliding to a stop in front of the livery, Will handed Tommy down to Bryce before dismounting. Grabbing his rifle, he swatted the horse with his hat to get it clear and ran into the building where Clay and Ben Johnson were waiting. Bullets began to smack into the walls as he ducked behind the door. Turning to face the men riding down on the town, he heard the roar of several rifles as the men on the building tops opened fire on the outlaws.

Three men were shot from their saddles in the first volley, but the rest of them never slowed. Half the men were crouched low over their horses, holding their torches out to the side. The rest of the men had rifles or pistols in hand and returned a withering fire into the buildings. There was a cry from the hotel, and Ben saw a man grab his chest and slump out of sight behind the signboard.

Shots continued to ring out from the men stationed among the buildings, but still the outlaws came on yelling, screaming, and shooting as fast as they could. Charging down the street, torches were flung onto roofs and into doorways where the flames could be seen trying to gain a foothold on the dry wood.

Nelson rode his horse towards the saloon, drawing his arm back to throw his torch through the batwing doors. Stepping through the doors as he pulled back the hammers, Art Delaware raised the ten gauge shotgun he was holding. The charge from the first barrel hit Nelson in the shoulder, shredding his arm and spinning him sideways in the saddle. The blast from the second barrel took him in the side, throwing his lifeless body off the horse and out into the street. Art walked over to the torch lying on the sidewalk and kicked it into the street beside the body of the dead outlaw. Calmly loading his shotgun again, Art looked over the street, waiting for the next outlaw to try and burn his saloon.

Bryce and Clay were at the windows in the livery firing at the attackers as they rode by. Clay had killed two men and Bryce another before the gang was past them. Stepping to the door of the livery, they continued to fire at the outlaws who were charging down the street, riding through a gauntlet of bullets from the tops of buildings and the doors and windows of the buildings whose owners had decided to fight.

In less than two minutes the fight was over, the outlaws fleeing past the hotel and turning up an alley next to the freight company. Nine outlaws lay dead in the dusty street, and from the look of them, several more had been injured. Clay knew that at least one townsman was dead but had no idea how many might have been injured.

"We did it! We done run 'em off!" shouted Ben, pumping his fist in the air. "That'll teach them bastards to mess with our town."

"Shut up you fool," snarled Clay. "We didn't run anyone off. They're just regrouping to hit us again. We bloodied them, and they weren't expecting that. They're going to want vengeance now, which makes them even more dangerous.

"Will, get some men together. Make sure they know how to shoot, and give them plenty of ammunition. We're going to have to go after them before they get re-organized and realize that there are plenty of hostages out there for them to take. Bryce, see if you and Sally can get over to the hotel and find out if that man is dead or wounded. Ben, take Hank and Sam and make your way over to the saloon 'n give Art a hand. Any wounded you find, try and get them to the hotel. They'll be safer there, and you can use tablecloths and sheets for bandages." Reloading his Remingtons, Clay turned to Will.

"They'll most likely try to get into the houses off the main street and come at us that way. If we get to the alley behind the bank, we can come up on their flank. They won't be able to move back into town with the rifles we have on the roof tops, and we can pin them down by the freight company." Checking that the four men with Will were ready, Clay pointed to the wagons in front of the building.

"Will and I will lay down some covering fire. When we start, you men run hard across the street for the bank. When you get there, start shooting towards the freight building, and we'll come across to join you." Nodding at Will, he looked carefully out the door and then crouched low and moved quickly to the nearest wagon with Will close behind.

Looking through the gap below the wagon's seat, Clay watched the freight building for a moment before he saw a flicker of movement near a stack of boxes. Rising up just enough to clear his gun hand, he began firing rapidly at the movement, fire lancing from the barrel. Will stood beside him, firing his Colt as fast as he could thumb the hammer back. There was a loud cry from the behind the boxes, and then a body slumped to the ground, a rifle clattering out to lie silent in the dirt.

The four men Will had picked ran low across the street and into the narrow alley next to the mercantile store, where they stopped and began to fire towards the outlaws. Putting a hand on Will's shoulder, Clay motioned towards the bank. Finished reloading, the two men crossed the street, firing as they went.

Moving quickly down the alley towards the hotel, Clay and his men could hear rifles firing from the tops of the jail, the saloon and the hotel, with answering fire still coming from the freight building. Reaching the street separating the mercantile from the hotel, they quickly crossed into the shadows behind the buildings.

****

While Clay was moving on the outlaws, Ben, Hank and Sam reached the back of the saloon. Opening the door into the rear storage room, they entered the saloon and moved towards the front. Ben opened the door to the main room and stepped through to find himself staring down the enormous barrels of Art's ten gauge double barrel.

"Dammit Ben, what the hell you tryin' to do sneakin' up a fella like that? I could've blown your fool head off!" Art was glaring hard at Ben as he slowly lowered the shotgun and turned back to the front windows.

"The outlaws are holed up behind the freight building," said Ben after getting his breath back. "Sorry, I shoulda hollered out it was us before I barged in like that. Anyway, Clay and some men are trying to get around behind them. If we can trap them there, maybe we can hold 'em off till help gets here from Ione."

Crouched behind a stake of wooden crates behind the freight building, Stewart was worried. Somehow the town had known he was coming and had found the backbone to make a stand. Half his gang was dead, several more wounded, and everyone was low on ammo. If they didn't get out of here soon, they were going to be surrounded

Turning to Bowden, struggling to reload his Winchester with his bad arm, Stewart pointed to the rear of the building. Get that door open. We're dead if we stay out here!"

Bowden put down his Winchester, turned to Frank and grabbed his shotgun with his good hand. He turned and fired both barrels at the lock, blowing a gaping hole in the door and the frame. Tossing the gun back, he grabbed his rifle and kicked the door open. Holding his wounded arm to his side, he ran inside followed closely by Stewart and the rest of the men still standing.

"Bowden, you stay here and keep watch. They'll try to get behind us, so make sure you look sharp. The rest of you, get to the front windows and see what the rest of these damn heroes are trying to do. I'll see if there's anything in here that might give us a chance to escape."

As his men obeyed his orders, Stewart began to move through the crates and boxes in the storage room, reading labels and swearing under his breath. Then he saw a small pile of boxes under a piece of canvas against the far wall. Picking up the edge, he read the label, a smile beginning to appear on his face as a plan began to form in his mind.

Chapter 23

Their horses all but done in, the posse was about a mile away from the town when they heard the gunfire and saw smoke rising above the trees.

"Come on men," yelled Sheriff Martin as he urged his tired horse on. "You can hear shots, means the town is still under attack. We still have a chance to save the town and catch Stewart and his men." Grimly the men pulled guns from holsters and scabbards and rode on, determined to save their friends and neighbors from the outlaws.

"It's Sheriff Martin and the posse!" cried out a man from the roof of the hotel.

"Sheriff Martin, they're holed up in the freight building!" Bryce hollered out to the Sheriff as his men reined in their horses and took cover behind boxes, wagons and doorways. The outlaws unleashed a barrage of fire from their hiding places, forcing everyone to take cover.

Dodging through the door to the saloon, Sheriff Martin found Sam and Ben Johnson at the windows, rifles in hand, firing rapidly at the outlaws. Art Delaware was sitting at a table, his shotgun and a bottle of whiskey by his hand. Hank was bent over Art tying a bloody cloth around his left shoulder.

"You alright, Art?" he asked.

"Yeah, I'm fine. Took one in the shoulder is all." Art grimaced as Hank finished his work and stepped back. Taking the bottle, Art tilted his head back and took a slug of the whiskey, then slammed the bottle back on the table.

"We got at least eight or nine of them bastards when they rode into town. Slim Jameson is dead, and a couple of Francis's men were killed. I think a couple was wounded. Sally's been taking care of them over to the hotel. They were carrying torches when they rode in, trying to set fire to the town. So far the only fires were small and easily put out."

"How'd you know they were coming, Ben?" asked Sheriff Martin. "We had no idea 'til we found the hideout empty and talked to the lookout they left behind."

"Old Loomer warned us. Seems Mr. Francis found out Loomer was sometimes taking game he'd killed up to the hideout and selling it to Stewart. He paid him to listen and then come back and tell him what he'd heard. Early this morning he rode into town and told Mr. Francis that Stewart was planning to burn us out. It was Mr. Francis that got things organized, putting men on the roofs and setting water barrels around town in case any fires did get started. Good thing we did, 'cause we was able to put out right quick the two that did get started."

"Well I'll be," said Martin. "Perhaps we've misjudged Clay. Where is he now?"

"He took some men over behind the hotel to try and get around behind Stewart. There was some shootin', and then we saw men moving inside the freight building."

****

Stewart had heard the commotion in the street and reached a window in the front of the building in time to see the Sheriff duck into the saloon. That meant the rest of the posse was back as well, and it was past time to get out of this damn town and take up business somewhere else.

"It's getting' too hot around here men. Time for us to leave."

"How we gonna do that with our hides intact?" asked Bowden.

"We got horses out back. All we gotta do is distract them for a bit, reach the horses and ride outta here."

"Ride where? You know they're gonna be after us as soon as we go out that door."

"Quit your whinin', Bowden. There's a load of dynamite under that canvas. I figure we pile it up against this front wall with a few barrels of that coal oil there. Pile a bunch of other stuff around it, then we get in back and light the fuse. The explosion and fire will keep 'em too busy to worry about following us."

"You outta your mind, Stewart?" Bowden's eyes were so big the whites were showing all the way around. "You wanna kill all of us with this stupid idea?" The panic was strong in Bowden's voice, and he was shaking so much he had to hold onto the door.

"So maybe we make it and maybe we don't. We stay here, we're dead. Keep watch here and let us know if anyone gets brave and tries to rush us."

Turning back to the front of the building, Stewart shouted orders to his men to start hauling the dynamite and coal oil to stack along the front wall. When that was done, he had them stack all the boxes they could move on top.

Finding a coil of fuse, Stewart cut a length he figured would give them about five minutes and had everyone take cover in the back room behind a large crate full of wrought iron parts. Looking out the window to make sure they weren't being rushed, he lit the fuse and scurried back with his men.

****

Watching the freight building from the alley behind the hotel, Clay and Will were talking quietly. They'd received word that Sheriff Martin had made it back to town; and that he and his men were scattered around buildings just down the street. That blocked the outlaws from trying to ride back out the way they'd come in. They couldn't go out the other end of town because there was no cover that way. Men stationed on the roof tops could gun them down before they got two hundred yards. If they tried the back of the building, Clay, Will and the others would pin them down before they could get to their horses. They were boxed in, and they had to know it.

"Will, send Elliot over to the Sheriff. Let him know they can't get out this way. Stewart himself wouldn't surrender, but maybe his men will give up if Martin talks to them." Clay had no qualms about killing the outlaws where they stood, but his sense of honor required that he try to at least offer them the chance to surrender. Turning back to watch the building, he wondered what them men over there might be doing.

Sheriff Martin was at the window of the saloon when he saw Elliot appear next to the saloon. The man waved to make sure they knew it was him and then waited for a sign from Ben before running across the street. Martin frowned when no shots came from the outlaws.

"They're up to something in there, Ben. I just don't know what it might be. Art, you have any ideas?"

"Not me, Sheriff," answered Art. "But I agree. They must be up to something, they've been quiet for a good twenty minutes now."

"Let's see if they might want to talk." Pushing away from the window, Martin walked to the edge of the doorway where he had a clear view of the front of the building. Across the way, unseen, Clay and Will stood up and raised their rifles as they saw a flicker of movement near the back door.

Taking a deep breath to call out to the outlaws, Sheriff Martin looked around the door frame just as the world exploded in a tremendous flash of fire and smoke. Windows exploded into the saloon and in other buildings all up and down the street. The shock wave from the blast threw Martin back into the saloon to land against the bar with a force that drove the air from his lungs.

Flying debris riddled the buildings around the freight office. One man was killed on the roof of the hotel when a flying board hit him in the neck almost taking his head completely off. Another suffered a broken arm and leg after being blown off the upper balcony of the saloon. Clay and Will were lifted from their feet and blown several feet back into the alley. They were alive only because the bulk of the blast had gone out the front of the building. In less than a second, the freight office was reduced to smoking rubble while flaming debris rained down on several buildings, starting several small fires.

After seeing that the Sheriff was alive, Ben ran out in the street and rounded up the dazed men.

"You men get buckets and start on those fires. See if you can find other folks to help you."

"What about the outlaws?" asked one.

"We'll take care of that. You men just get those fires out. I don't think anyone in there could have survived, but we'll check it out."

Staggering dazed to his feet, Clay shook his head to clear it and looked up just in time to see three figures run out of the back of the destroyed building. Running over to the panicked horses, they struggled to mount the pitching animals. Finally able to get enough control to get in the saddles, they whipped their horses into a gallop, quickly disappearing south into the trees.

"We gonna follow them, Clay?" asked Will, holding a bandana to the cut in his scalp.

"No. I seriously doubt they're planning to come back. We need to see who's been hurt and make sure we get all these fires out. We could still lose the town if they get out of control." Holstering his pistol, Clay looked around for his hat. Picking it up, he brushed it off quickly and put it on before walking briskly around the corner towards the street.

Chapter 24

Bigsby and his friends had just come out of a small draw, the road into town visible through the brush ahead, when the sound rolled down the valley.

"What's that? Thunder?" asked Tom.

"No, sounded more like an explosion, an' a big one," answered Calaveras.

"That came from town, look there!" said Bigsby as he pointed at a column of smoke appearing over the ridge ahead. "Something bad's happened. C'mon!" Putting the spurs to his horse, Bigsby lead his friends toward the smoke hanging in the sky over the town.

Rather than follow the road, they headed on as straight a line as they could towards the town, hoping to save time and get there soon enough to be of help. Their horses seemed to sense the urgency of their riders; and, tired as they were, responded to the commands for even more speed. Crashing through brush and ducking under the branches of the live oak and digger pine trees, they crossed a small ridge and dropped down into the narrow tree filled valley on the other side. Reaching the bottom, they had to slow their horses to a trot in the thick underbrush.

Crossing as quickly as they could, they scrambled their horses up the far side. The loose soil was sliding under their horses hooves, making the climb slow and treacherous.

From the top of the ridge, the men could see they were about two miles from town. One smaller valley lay ahead of them before they were out of the trees and into the low brush and grass of the central valley. Urging their horses, the men rode down into the trees, leaving a cloud of red in the air behind them.

John was leading the way with Bigsby and Calaveras close behind, followed by Tom Morris, when they heard the sound of running horses ahead. Using hand signals, John indicated a stand of trees to the right; and the men quickly rode their horses under the concealing branches. They had barely gotten out of sight when three men came into sight a hundred yards away. Riding at a full gallop, they were leaning low over their horse's necks, most likely to avoid being knocked off by a low branch.

"That's Stewart!" yelled John as he grabbed for his rifle. Before he could get off a shot, the fleeing outlaws had ridden out of sight in the trees.

"John, you and Tom get to town. See what you can do to help. Tell Sheriff Martin that Calaveras and I have gone after Stewart and to follow us when he can," Bigsby said.

"You sure you don't need us to stay with you?" asked Tom.

"We can handle them," said Bigsby. "From the sound of that explosion, I think they can use you two in town."

"Alright, we'll find the Sheriff and have him follow you. Be careful."

"We will. Come on Calaveras, we have a couple of runaways to round up."

"No need to hurry," said Calaveras. "From the looks of those horses, if they don't slow down soon, they'll be on foot." Nodding to Tom and John, Calaveras moved off at a slow trot with Bigsby towards where they had seen the fleeing outlaws disappear.

Reaching the spot where they'd last seen the outlaws, Bigsby and Calaveras found their trail easy to follow, the tracks from the running horses having cut deeply into the soft dirt.

"That one's already starting to falter," said Calaveras, pointing to one set of tracks. "You can see the stride isn't consistent, and there it almost went down before it caught itself. I figure less than half a mile and they'll have to slow down."

"Is there any place in particular around here they might be running to?" asked Bigsby, watching the trail as they moved along at a trot.

"Nothing that stands out in my mind. You have to understand that there're caves, abandoned mines and such all over these hills. They could be headed anywhere."

"Remember what Dusty told us? He said that Stewart was moving things to another hideout."

"That's right. Didn't he say that some fella named Jeeter, I think it was, and two or three other guys had already left?"

"Guess we'd better try and catch up to them before they get wherever it is they think their going, hadn't we?"

"You have a point, Bigsby. Wouldn't do to give them four to one odds, now would it?"

"No Sir, Calaveras. Wouldn't be fair to them at all." The banter was the comfortable exchange between old friends, but their faces showed they were serious about what they had to do.

****

Handsome was almost an hour behind the Sheriff and his posse. When the sound of the explosion from the town reached them, the horse had panicked into a run, almost overturning the carriage before Handsome got it back under control. Dusty had taken advantage of the distraction and had made a break for it, forcing Handsome to finally take his rifle and send a shot past Dusty's ear before he stopped running. Hands in the air, Dusty had looked quite miserable as he walked back to the carriage.

"Dusty, I'm afraid you could never make your way in proper society," he told the outlaw as he tied a rope around his body before looping it through the seat back and under the seat itself. Stepping back from the job, he brushed off his clothes and retrieved his hat from the rock where he'd left it.

"You gave me your word you wouldn't try to escape before we started out, and I expected you to keep it, as any gentlemen would. I now realize that you were acting falsely, attempting to win your freedom through deception. You obviously assumed that I would be lulled by your acquiescence to the point of laxness, thereby allowing you to extricate yourself from a very untenable situation."

Dusty could only stare at Handsome for several moments, his mouth working silently. Finally, shaking his head he blurted out, "What in tarnation did you just say? Just, just, shut up talkin' in them big words like that. My heads so rattled up I can't think straight anymore."

"I sincerely doubt that 'thinking straight', as you refer to it, ever took very much of your time," said Handsome. "Alright, in language perhaps even someone such as you might understand, this is what I said. You lied to me when you promised not to run, thinking I would not watch you closely. You know you are in a great deal of trouble and wanted to escape, taking responsibility for your actions by running away."

"Huh?" asked Dusty.

"You tried to escape, you miserable little man, and you're very fortunate I don't just shoot you now and leave you here!" shouted Handsome, finally losing his temper. Scowling darkly at his captive, he climbed into his seat on the carriage and picked up the short whip. Favoring Dusty with another disgusted look, he snapped the reins and started the carriage towards town. He'd been acting upset with his prisoner to hide his own fear.

The explosion he'd heard had been a very large one. He was certain they were going to find something awful had happened in town.

Chapter 25

Sheriff Martin was back on his feet by the time Ben and Clay came back into the saloon. The fires had fortunately all been small and by now most had been put out. The wounded, fortunately a small number, had been taken to the hotel where Sally Standeford was directing their care.

"Hello, Sheriff," said Clay as he walked through the doorway. "Glad to see you're alright."

"Yeah, I'm fine. What's it like out there?" Martin asked Ben. He was still shaky but determined to take control of the situation.

"Well, the freight office is gone, nothing left but a large hole and a lot of debris scattered all over town. The corrals behind the freight office were knocked down by panicked livestock, and there's a lot of damage to the nearby buildings. Most of that is minor, windows blown out, doors broken, that sort of thing. It shouldn't take too long to fix things up."

"Luke West and Adam Beale are dead and Jim Deering has several broken bones from being blown off the roof by the explosion," said Clay. "Several others were wounded but not seriously. We killed nine of Stewart's men before they took cover in the freight office. I'm not sure how many were in there, but I can tell you that only three made it out alive after the explosion."

"You can't be serious. No one could have survived that!" Disbelief was evident on Martin's face as he looked out the window at the smoking ruin down the street.

"I'm afraid so, Sheriff. I believe one of them was Stewart, though with all the smoke I can't be sure. They got to the horses and rode south out of town." Clay pulled a bottle of whiskey off the bar and poured three glasses. Handing one each to Ben and Sheriff Martin, he raised his glass.

"We were lucky today, Sheriff. Let's drink to that." Tossing back the whiskey, Clay sat his glass on the bar. "Sheriff," he said as he picked up his hat and walked to the door.

"What're you going to do, Mr. Francis?" asked Ben.

"I'm going to check with my men and see if everyone is all right. Sheriff, I don't think Stewart would be foolish enough to come back, but I also believe we need to track him down. Let me know when, and I will join you in the search. Whether he stands trial for his crimes I will leave up to you."

****

Handsome was uncharacteristically silent as he entered Murieta with his prisoner. He'd expected it to be bad when he saw all the smoke rising from several places in town and when he'd come across the bodies of the outlaws killed in the attack. But he wasn't prepared for the carnage he saw as he turned onto the main street and the results of the explosion the outlaws had set off to make their escape came into view. Debris covered the street, and folks were carrying one body towards the undertakers while another was being put on a small wagon. Driving the carriage slowly down the street, he pulled up in front of the saloon, worried about his friend Art.

Leaving Dusty tied to the seat, Handsome hurriedly climbed down and ran towards the saloon. Jumping up on the boardwalk, he could see Art just inside the door, picking up a chair knocked over when the windows blew in.

"Art, are you okay?" he asked.

"I'm okay, Handsome, but as you can see the Gold Creek is quite a bit worse for wear." Reaching for the broom nearby, he began to sweep some of the glass into a pile near the door, his wounded shoulder making it a hard job. "It'll take a lot of money to fix this place up again. I'll be able to get most of the window glass from Sacramento, but I'll probably have to go to San Francisco to get a new mirror."

"Is Penny alright? She's not hurt is she?" As he talked, Handsome was moving around the saloon, picking up tables and chairs and setting them back upright.

"No, Penny's fine, though as you can imagine she's pretty mad about all this. She'd just gotten the place the way she liked it, and now most of the curtains and table cloths will need to be replaced. I know she's going to have me re-painting the inside before she's done." Art picked a broken bottle off the floor, and then sadly added it to the growing pile of debris. "Lost most of the stock behind the bar, but that's about it."

"Did they get Stewart? And where's Sheriff Martin? I have a prisoner out front."

"From what Ben and Clay Francis were saying, Stewart got away with two of his men. Sheriff Martin and Ben are around here somewhere. They were checking on damage and injuries. Take your prisoner on over to the jail. He'll be there eventually." Art lit a cigar, and giving Handsome a wave, slowly began scoping the pile of broken glass he'd collected into a bucket he brought out from behind the bar.

"As soon as I have this villain behind bars, I'll be back to help clean up, Art, I promise." Climbing back on the carriage, Handsome turned the rig around and headed back to the jail, where he untied his cowering prisoner and marched him inside. Finding the keys to the cells, he put Dusty in the closest one and locked the door.

"If I were you, I'd just sit there and be very quiet," he told Dusty.

He walked back into the office, hung the keys on the peg behind the desk and closed the outer door as he left. Keeping his word to Sally, he returned the undamaged vehicle to the livery where he unhitched and turned out the horse before walking back to the saloon to help his friend. At the same time he was wondering what Calaveras and Bigsby were doing.

****

Before Bigsby and Calaveras had gone the half mile predicted, they saw the change in the trail they followed.

"They've slowed their horses, probably moving about the same speed we are now," said Bigsby. "Don't think we'll catch up to them before dark."

"I expect you're right, Bigsby. Desperate as they are right now, we'd be asking to get ambushed if we try to take them," answered Calaveras.

"Let's stay with the trail until dark then make camp. If they want to stumble around in the dark, that's up to them. We'll start after them again at first light."

"Good idea. Besides, if they don't know we're this close, they may not be in such a hurry."

Three hours later Bigsby called a halt. "I figure they can't be more than a couple miles ahead of us now," he told his friend as they stopped in the shelter of a couple large trees. "Let's water the horses over there and then stake them out. You have any food with you?"

"Couple strips of jerky is all, you?"

"Same here. looks like a pretty boring meal tonight."

"Leastways it's something to eat. I don't do too well on grass or bark, you know."

Stripping the gear from their mounts, the two men carried it to the base of the trees. Once the horses had their fill of water, they staked the animals nearby so they could graze on the grass growing along the stream.

"What do plan to do once we catch them, Bigsby?" asked Calaveras.

"I've been thinking about that, Calaveras. For what he did to my folks, I'd like to shoot him on sight." Calaveras watched his friend struggle with his anger before he was able to continue. "While he might deserve that, it would make me just as bad as him if I did. He's a thief and a murderer, but he needs to be brought to trial before a judge. We have laws in this land, and while Stewart chose not to follow them, I did. I'll try to take him alive, but I won't be afraid to shoot if I have to."

"I was hoping you'd feel that way, Bigsby. You get some rest. I'll take the first watch."

Chapter 26

Dawn was just touching the tops of the nearby hills, the dew flashing into thin clouds of steam as the suns rays hit. Finishing his cigarette, Bigsby walked over and nudged Calaveras awake.

"Time to get after it," he said as his friend stretched before getting to his feet. Working with practiced ease, the two men quickly packed their gear and saddled their horses. Less than ten minutes later they were once more on the trail of Stewart and the other two men.

Forty-five minutes later they came to the remains of a small fire. From the signs left behind, they figured they were less than an hour behind them. A bloody rag dropped by the edge of the clearing gave evidence that at least one of them had been injured.

"An injured man might slow 'em down some," commented Calaveras.

"Could do that," answered Bigsby. "Might also cost the fellow his life if Stewart thinks they can go faster without him."

"You're right, it could. From what I hear, Stewart wouldn't hesitate to kill someone he thought was slowin' him down." Calaveras circled the small clearing and picked up the trail again. "They're still headed south. Only thing I know down this way that's close is Whitman's Quarry."

"I remember. Weren't they taking limestone out of there?"

"Yeah, fellow name of Whitman was selling the limestone to builders in Sacramento and San Francisco. Did pretty well for a while 'til he hit an underground stream. It flooded the quarry faster than pumps could cope with. He shut it down a few years ago and moved his operations down south somewhere. There were several caves nearby, but I didn't think they were very big."

"How far is it from here, you think?" asked Bigsby.

"Four, five miles maybe. I've never actually seen the place, just heard about it.

"If that's where his new hideout is, we better catch them before they get there." Tapping his horses ribs with his spurs, Bigsby set off at a canter along the clear trail left by the fleeing men.

They'd only gone about a mile when the sound of a single shot echoed through the hills ahead of them. Reining in their horses, Bigsby and Calaveras listened intently.

"They can't be more 'n a few hundred yards ahead of us now. We need to move slow and spread out," said Bigsby. "I'll stay on the trail. You move off about fifty yards east. They won't be able to take us both at once, and maybe we'll be able to spot any ambush they might plan."

Calaveras pulled his rifle from it's scabbard and levered a round into the chamber. Nodding to Bigsby, he quietly moved off the trail until he was separated by forty or fifty yards. One at a time Bigsby pulled his Colts and checked the loads. Re-holstering the pistols, he pulled his Winchester and levered in a round, then loaded another to keep the magazine full. Picking up the reins in his left hand, he started slowly forward, watching closely for any sign of a trap.

Rounding a bend in the trail, Bigsby saw a rider less horse on the trail ahead. Pulling back, he motioned to Calaveras. Watching carefully, he could see that the horse was interested in something ahead. Rather than grazing it was standing still, head up and ears forward as it watched a large pile of rocks that stood to one side of the trail perhaps seventy-five yards further ahead. Moving forward a few feet, Bigsby saw a body on the ground near the trail. Obviously dead from the way the arms and legs were splayed out, he figured it was most likely the injured man, shot because he couldn't keep up.

Motioning Calaveras, he pointed to the pile of rocks and then indicated that he would circle to the right through the trees. Calaveras nodded and moved ahead to his left, keeping some brush between himself and the rocks.

Dismounting slowly, Bigsby dropped the reins of his horse, which immediately lowered its head to graze. Moving quietly, he began to move towards the rocks. He had covered about half the distance when he saw a flicker of movement near the top, maybe forty feet above the trail. Watching carefully, he stepped around a deadfall of branches and began to move forward again, stepping carefully to avoid twigs and leaves on the ground.

"Hello, Bigsby. Didn't expect it to be you." The harsh voice stopped Bigsby in his tracks. Stewart had him cold.

"Drop the rifle, Bigsby. Now!" Bigsby could hear tones in the voice he didn't like at all. Stewart had been pushed beyond reasoning. He felt wronged and intended to kill everyone he felt was responsible. Dropping the rifle, Bigsby slowly raised his hands, wondering if he'd hear the shot he expected to tear into his back at any second.

"Turn around slow, Bigsby. Wouldn't want folks sayin' I shot a man in the back. Nope, that just wouldn't do at all, now would it?"

Obeying, Bigsby slowly turned to face Stewart. He was standing about ten feet away, a Colt .44 in his hand aimed at Bigsby's chest. Looking at the gun, Bigsby saw the hammer was cocked. If he tried to jump Stewart now he'd be dead before he moved two feet.

Looking Stewart over, Bigsby realized the outlaw was in bad shape. His jeans and shirt were covered in soot, and several large tears and burns were evident on his arms and legs. He was bleeding from several cuts and scrapes, as well as his left ear. His left eye was almost swollen shut, and looking back at the gun, Bigsby could see that it was beginning to shake slightly.

"You don't look so good, Stewart," he said. "I was you, I'd be thinking I need a Doctor. You hand over that gun, and we'll see that you get one."

"You want to fix me up so I'll live long enough to hang is all. I ain't that stupid, Bigsby. All I have to do is kill you; and I can ride out of here. I'll find a friendly Doc somewhere's and get myself patched up."

"Maybe, if I'd come out here by myself, that would be true. " The gun was shaking a little more now, the strain of holding it up beginning to take a toll on the exhausted Stewart. If he could keep him talking a bit longer, maybe he'd have a chance.

"You said you weren't stupid, Stewart; so surely you don't think I'm out here alone. You shoot me and the others will know where you are. Your horses are done. You're barely able to stand and you wouldn't get far before they'd run you down."

"Lyin' ain't gonna save you, Bigsby. I know you wasn't with the posse. Was just bad luck on my part you stumbled across my trail. Or perhaps the bad luck was yours, since I'm the one holdin' the gun." Stewart licked his lips nervously as he quickly shifted his grip on the Colt. "I want you to use your right hand and slowly unbuckle that gunbelt and let it drop.'

"You going to shoot an unarmed man, Stewart? Of course you would. Anyone cowardly enough to shoot an injured partner wouldn't hesitate to shoot a man with out a gun, would they?" As he talked, Bigsby was slowly moving his right hand towards the buckle on his gun belt.

"He was slowin' us down. Couldn't stay on his horse."

"So you shot him, one of your own men." Keeping his eyes on the gun, Bigsby moved his fingers as if he was trying to unfasten the buckle on his gun belt.

"He was dead anyway. Something from the explosion hit him in the stomach, tore him up bad inside. I just made it quick for him." Stewart was acting strange, like something was wrong with his eyes. He kept rubbing his face and shaking his head like he was trying to shake something off.

"I said drop that gunbelt now! Hurry up!" shouted Stewart. Raising the gun he had pointed at Bigsby to eye level, he took a step forward.

Bigsby finally unhooked his gunbelt and let it drop to his feet. Moving slowly, he pushed it to the side with his foot where it would be out of the way when he made his move. Stewart was shaking badly. If he could just find a way to distract him.

Just then two shots rang out from near the rocks, causing Stewart to start violently and swing his pistol away from Bigsby. Immediately Bigsby seized his chance and rushed Stewart, throwing himself at his legs in an effort to bring him down.

Seeing Bigsby coming at him, Stewart swung the Colt back and fired just as Bigsby crashed into him. Knocked backwards to the ground, the pistol flew from his hand and landed several feet away. Pulling his legs against his chest, Stewart kicked out hard, catching Bigsby in the side and knocking him away.

Scrambling to his feet, Stewart looked wildly around for the gun before seeing it lying near some rocks. Lunging for the pistol, he felt Bigsby grab his arm. Turning, he swung a roundhouse punch that Bigsby blocked with his left arm while landing a solid punch to Stewart's stomach. Doubled up from the blow, Stewart staggered away, still trying to reach his gun.

Seeing what Stewart was trying to reach, Bigsby dove for Stewarts leg's and tripped him up before he could reach the weapon. Scrabbling on the ground, Stewart's hands closed on a fist-sized rock. Grabbing hold, he rolled over and swung it at Bigsby, catching him in the forehead.

Stunned, Bigsby let go of Stewart and rolled away. He'd managed to get to his hands and knees when Stewart, forgetting about the gun, delivered a vicious kick to his ribs. Before Bigsby could catch his breath or move out of the way, Stewart kicked him again. Bigsby felt a rib break as he was driven onto his back by the blow. He lay there, barely conscious, as Stewart, breathing hard, started towards his gun.

Rolling slowly onto his side, Bigsby realized that he had fallen next to his dropped gun belt. Reaching out, the pain from his injured side stabbed his chest, turning his vision red. Fighting to stay conscious he reached the gun and started to pull his gun free when he saw Stewart pick up his gun and spin to face Bigsby, the desire to kill clearly on his face. Pulling the trigger, he fired, his shot hitting the dirt only inches from Bigsby's head.

With no time to draw, Bigsby lifted his holstered gun and fired. The heavy slug caught Stewart in the shoulder, shattering the joint and spinning him to the ground.

Holding an arm to his side to ease the pain of broken bones, Bigsby slowly made his way to his feet, keeping his eyes on Stewart. The outlaw, wounded but still alive, was cursing weakly, pulling himself along the ground, his useless arm trailing behind him as he again tried to reach his gun. Walking slowly, Bigsby reached the fallen pistol first and picked it up. Tucking it in his belt, he looked at the wounded man in front of him.

"Give it up Stewart. It's over now," he said.

Rolling over onto his back, Stewart looked up at Bigsby and spat. "So go ahead and shoot me, Bigsby. Get it over with. Come on," he shouted. "You know you want to. You know it was my men that attacked your Ma and Pa. I hear they messed your Ma up pretty good too. Shoulda told 'em to kill 'em instead of just roughing them up."

"You're right, Stewart, I should shoot you like the rabid dog you really are." Looking at the helpless man on the ground, Bigsby was fighting the rage he felt inside, his fingers turning white from the force of his grip on the gun.

"Well, what are you waiting for, ya coward?" Using his feet, Stewart pushed himself along to a nearby rock where he could use his good arm to push his body into a sitting position facing Bigsby.

Calaveras had arrived at the scene unnoticed by either man. Standing only a few feet away, he could clearly see the struggle his friend was going through.

"Think about what you want to do, Bigsby," he said. "Stewart's trying to get you to shoot for two reasons. He knows he's not getting out of this, and he'd much rather die quick by a bullet than get hauled into court, tried, and then hung. Can't say as I blame him, but that's not for us to decide. That's his other reason. He gets you to kill him and that makes you an outlaw too. You shoot an unarmed man, and no matter what the reason, you're a murderer."

Bigsby heard what his friend was saying and knew he was right. Much as he wanted to, it wasn't up to him to decide if the man should live or die. Remembering what he'd told Calaveras last night, Bigsby felt the red haze of his anger fade. Lowering his gun, he looked at Stewart.

"Calaveras is right, you know. Killing you lets you off easy. That's not going to happen. We're going to patch you up and deliver you to the Sheriff. The law is going to decide your fate, Stewart, not me." Turning to his friend, Bigsby nodded his thanks.

"What about the other guy he was with? You take care of him?"

"Yeah, I've got him tied up over by the rocks. He took a bullet in the shoulder like your friend here, but he'll live long enough to hang."

"It was your shooting that distracted Stewart enough to give me a chance. I made a mistake, and he had me cold. Don't know why he didn't shoot when he had the chance. Guess he wanted to brag about himself before he killed me." Moving to the injured man, Bigsby removed his shirt and tore it into strips. Rolling some of the strips into a pad, he tied the rough bandage around his shoulder.

Pulling Stewart to his feet, Calaveras held him while Bigsby fetched a short piece of rope from his horse. Pulling the outlaws hands together, he tied them quickly and stepped back.

"Take him over to the base of the rocks. You'll find his partner there. While you're doing that, I'll round up their horses so they don't have to walk all the way back to town."

****

Bigsby walked his prisoner over to the rocks and had him sit down near the other one. Finding a handy boulder, he leaned against it to ease the pain of his ribs while he watched them. He'd finally managed to get a smoke rolled and lit when Calaveras rode up leading the outlaws' horses.

"Time to mount up, boys," he called. Dismounting, he led the horses over to the captives. Bigsby helped him haul them to their feet, ignoring their cries and curses about their injuries. "Come on, get on those horses."

"How you expect me to mount a horse with my hands tied?" whined Stewart. "I can't raise my arms."

"You can ride back to town sitting in the saddle or tied across it, doesn't matter much to me," answered Calaveras.

"You gonna shoot us cause we can't get on a horse?" cried the other captive.

"Didn't say anything about shooting anybody," said Calaveras. "You don't want to mount up, I'll just knock you out and tie you face down across the saddle. Your choice."

"Like hell you will," spat Stewart. Jerking away from Bigsby's grip on his arm, he started to run for the trees.

Taking two long strides, Calaveras cut off the fleeing man. One short hard punch to the jaw and Stewart hit the ground out cold.

"Now where do you suppose he thought he was going?" asked Calaveras.

"Don't know the answer, but I do know he's going to be mighty disappointed when he wakes up." Bigsby was shaking his head in wonder at what he'd seen.

Picking the man up and putting him over his shoulder, Calaveras carried him over to his horse. Throwing him across the saddle, he used another piece of rope to ties his hands and feet together under the horse's belly.

"I figure that's going to hurt a lot worse than if he was sitting in the saddle, but it was his choice." Straightening up, Calaveras looked at the other captive. "So what's your choice? Sitting, or face down like you friend here?"

"Give me a boost up. I ain't gonna be taken into town like that." Walking unsteadily to his horse, Calaveras grabbed him by the belt and lifted him into his saddle.

Calaveras mounted his horse and took the reins of the outlaws horses. Walking his mount over to Bigsby, he handed him the reins of Stewart's horse.

"Shall we go see what's been happening in town while we were gone?" he asked.

As the two men lead their captives back towards town, Bigsby looked at his friend. "Thanks Calaveras. I wasn't sure if I could stop myself from shooting him for what he did."

"Don't know as I would've blamed you if you had, but I know you would've blamed yourself. Figured I'd just point that out and let you decide. Seems to me you made the right one and that's the end of it."

"Well, just wanted to say thanks anyway," replied Bigsby.

Chapter 27

The sun had set and lanterns and oil lamps were being lit all over town when Bigsby and Calaveras rode in with their prisoners. Word spread quickly through town of their arrival; and, by the time they reached the jail, a crowd was gathering in the street.

"Is that Stewart?" one man asked. "Is he dead?"

"No, he's not dead," answered Bigsby. Dismounting, he looped the reins over the rail and turned to his prisoner. Reaching under the horse, he untied the rope, then stood and pushed Stewart off the saddle and into the dirt street. Calaveras grabbed the collar of the outlaw's shirt, hauled him roughly to his feet, then walked him into the jail and headed for the cells.

"Where's the Sheriff, Ben?" he asked as he grabbed the keys and shoved Stewart into an empty cell and locked the door. Tossing the keys to Bigsby, he walked back into the office while Bigsby was locking Stewart and the other prisoner into their cells.

"Sheriff's over to the hotel with Bryce," answered Ben. "Sally's been helping with the wounded. We lost Slim Jameson, and Jim Deering got busted up pretty bad. Two of Mr. Francis's men, Adam Beale and Luke West, was killed too."

"Sally's taking care of the wounded? Where's Doc Barton?" asked Calaveras.

"Doc's dead. They found him yesterday morning. At first they thought he'd died in his sleep, but last I heard the Sheriff thinks he was murdered. He'd been drinkin' the night before, and some folks said they thought the man he was talkin' to was one of Stewart's men."

"That must be how Stewart found out we were coming, Bigsby," said Calaveras.

"Don't see how, 'cause your Pa killed him right after he left the saloon Bigsby." Ben was looking pretty uncomfortable as he gave out this bit of news.

"Where's Pa now, Ben? Is he alright?" Bigsby was headed for the door when Ben stopped him.

"Your Pa's fine. Turns out there was a Wanted Dead or Alive out for Sturgis. When you Pa tried to turn himself in, the Sheriff told him to just go on home and take care of Becca."

"Pa said he'd found out who ordered the attack and was looking for him. I guess he found him alright. I see Dusty's here, so I assume Handsome made it back in one piece?" asked Bigsby.

"Sure did," said Ben. "He's over to the saloon with Art. Said if you ever made it back to meet him there."

"I think we'll just do that. Ben. Thanks. Care to let me buy you a drink, Calaveras?" Bigsby was smiling as he opened the door for his friend.

"Don't mind if you do," he answered. "Ben, make damn sure you don't lose those prisoners. Bigsby and I are going over to the saloon, and I imagine a bottle or two might be in jeopardy of becoming empty."

Handsome looked up as his two friends walked into the saloon. "As usual gentlemen, your timing is atrocious. Once again you manage to make yourselves scarce until all the excitement Is over, and then waltz through the door as if everything was now normal because you've graced us with you divine presence."

"Handsome, you never change," said Bigsby. "Pompous as ever. That's what I like about you!" Grinning now, Bigsby walked over and hugged Handsome hard. Wriggling out of his friends grasp, Handsome hurriedly straightened himself and poured a drink for the two men.

"John and Tom told us you'd taken off after Stewart and his men. I gather from your presence here that you were successful in your endeavors?"

"Yes we were, Handsome, yes we were. Stewart and one of his men are in jail. The third one Stewart shot because he was wounded and slowing them down." Taking the offered drink from his friend, Bigsby raised his glass. "We got lucky today, no doubt about it. But the bad guys are in jail, and we're still standing." Tossing back his drink, Bigsby slapped Handsome on the shoulder and held out his glass.

"Come on, Handsome, stop hiding that bottle and Calaveras 'n I'll tell you how we captured Jesse Stewart."

"And no doubt it will be a tale fraught with daring-do and absolute fabrications," replied Handsome, pouring another round.

"No doubt at all, Handsome. Let's grab some chairs, and we'll tell you all about it!"

www.ingramcontent.com/pod-product-compliance
Lightning Source LLC
Chambersburg PA
CBHW020438180626
46812CB00003B/1292